C000039276

CLUELESS IN CROATIA

Joy Skye

Copyright © 2021 Joy Skye

All rights reserved

The characters and events portrayed in this book are fictitious.
Any similarity to real persons, living or dead, is coincidental
and not intended by the author.

No part of this book may be reproduced, or stored in a retrieval
system, or transmitted in any form or by any means, electronic,
mechanical, photocopying, recording, or otherwise, without
express written permission of the publisher.

Cover artwork by Gabriella Guy

*For my girls, a constant source of inspiration
and Mum, I hope you're enjoying this!*

CONTENTS

Title Page

Copyright

Dedication

THE STING   1

HOLIDAY   29

BIG SHOT   53

THE CAPTAIN   78

BEYOND THE SEA   100

CRAZY HORSES   125

FAMILY AFFAIR   149

LONDON CALLING   175

YESTERDAY   200

FEELS LIKE HOME   226

HAPPY EVER AFTER   239

Afterword   243

Books In This Series   245

Keep in Touch   247

THE STING

From: peterwilliams@sublimeretreats.com
To: angelica@staragents.co.uk
Subject: Promo

Dear Ms. Dickens,

Further to our telephone conversation this morning, please find attached a list of the villas available to host one of your celebrities.

As discussed, we would like them to experience a typical holiday with our club and promote the benefits of our membership and travelling with us in a positive light on Instagram.

As well as the villa, we will provide a hire car, the concierge service and would also like them to experience:

- Local excursions such as a boat trip/horse riding
- In house chef service
- In house spa treatments

The idea being that they can show all these extras being enjoyed as the week progresses.
Please let me know who you feel would be suitable. Our main requirement being that they have over

150,000 followers and are regular contributors.

I look forward to hearing from you, please note this is urgent as it is coming to the close of season in our European destinations.

Best regards,

Peter Williams
Sublime Retreats

L eonard Lupine slammed his front door shut with a snarl, causing the knocker to rattle alarmingly in protest. The popping paparazzi continued to pointlessly aim their cameras at the resolutely closed hunk of wood, for a good half hour after his disappearance, just in case.

Leaning, panting, against the dingy wall of his hallway, he shook off his infamous trench coat with practiced ease and threw it to the ground in disgust; he hated his daily dog fight with the packs of reporters that camped outside his front door. Speed dialing his agent as he strode through to the kitchen, phone wedged between shoulder and ear, he grabbed the carton of open grape juice from his retro style Smeg fridge and glugged it down straight, fervently wishing he could add vodka to it.

'Angelica,' he barked when she answered, 'I've had enough of this shit. Cancel my contract with Brava TV, I am not continuing with this ridiculous persona for another minute!'

There was a pause. He could hear her dragging on her oversized opalescent vape and imagined its hated swirls of mock smoke escaping around her gleaming head like something akin to Alice in wonderland.

'Have you finished?' came the drawling tones he'd come to loathe so much.

'Yes, I've bloody finished, that's what I am telling you. I can't do this anymore' he restated angrily, slamming the juice carton on the counter and ignoring the fountain of liquid that slopped out of the spout and spread across the granite work surface like diluted blood.

'There, there, Leo,' she mused absently, her mind apparently on things other than her number one star's current crisis. 'You and I both know that without Detective Fierce, you would be nothing.' Hearing the familiar mantra made his hackles rise and the fact she called him Leo, yet again, aggravated him further. Subconsciously rubbing the back of his neck, he took a long, calming breath before replying.

'But I could be something else; you know I want to produce my songs. I'd happily give this shit up to lock myself away in a studio somewhere and to hell with the rest of it,' he declared petulantly, pacing as far as his tiny, highly-functional, galley kitchen would allow before spinning around smartly and repeating the process.

In her chic, if chaotic, office in Denmark Street, the familiar, Doppler sounds of sirens in the distance, Angelica sat up straight, causing her throne-like chair to pivot. She was used to his despairing outbursts, but once in a while she knew she had to throw him a bone to keep him under control. She had worked far too hard for too long on his character to let him fly the coop just yet. Brain racing in hyper-drive, she smiled enigmatically, one perfectly plucked eyebrow arched.

'I tell you what' she began, shuffling swiftly through a pile of paperwork on her desk and causing a minor landslide on the far side 'how about a holiday?'

Startled, Leonard stopped mid pace, his angular frame looking stork-like as he paused with one leg bent. 'What on earth are you talking about? Did you not hear what I said?' he demanded.

'Of course I did, darling, but I think what you need most of all is a break, a little time away to relax, write some of your silly songs where you can't be disturbed.'

Filing the word 'silly' away for later retribution, he considered his agent's proposal. It did have a certain appeal, and he couldn't remember the last time he had been away anywhere. It was probably that ridiculous charade that had passed for a honeymoon.

'What did you have in mind?' he asked cautiously, not yet ready to give too much credence to her scheme.

'I'm being pestered by this company, hang on a minute... ah yes, here it is. Yes, a company called Sublime Retreats, looking to host one of my bigger stars in exchange for some promo, you know, a few arty beach shots on Insta, that kind of thing?'

'I'm not sure they want a grumpy old git like me promoting them. That sounds far more like my charming ex-wife's forte than mine.'

Not wanting to tell him that she had already asked the popular pop star sensation that was his ex-wife but she was far too busy and besides, a plan was forming in her ever devious mind that would help her achieve yet more limelight for all concerned.

'I was thinking it might be an opportunity for you to take the boys away for a few days. I'm sure Rennie will agree if it's organised through the firm.' She remarked nonchalantly, the hissing of her vape clearly coming down the line.

His tone immediately softened, and she knew she had won yet again. A smirk of satisfaction appeared on her face, causing her crow's feet to bunch up alarmingly.

'Well, if you think that's possible, of course I will go. I don't want it splattered all over the news, though. We have to have some privacy. How much promotion is this company looking for exactly?'

'Leave it all to me, darling,' she replied soothingly, rapidly typing out her response to Sublime Retreats as they spoke. 'I'll take care of all the details; you don't have to worry about a thing. They have properties all over. Some of them are quite remote by the looks of things. I'll pick somewhere inaccessible and we can delay your Insta feed for a day or two. By the time the paps work out where you and the kids are, you'll be on a flight home '

Putting the phone down gleefully, she stared out of the window for a moment, whilst she formulated the rest of her scheme. Then, deciding she'd earned it, shouted through to her beleaguered P.A. to go and get some coffee.

☼

Isabella, hearing the nagging tone heralding an email, picked up her phone, bangles dancing down her arm in protest, with lips pressed together in a hard line. It was nearly the end of the summer season on the small island of Brač, and she was exhausted. It had been full on all summer, and she was more than ready to curl up in front of the fire with a good book.

As a single mum to an energetic toddler, juggling work and motherhood these last few months had been exhausting. She smiled as Luka thundered past the balcony doors, pretending to be a plane, his passage causing her wind chimes to dance and peel their plaintive tinkles.

As she read through the email from Sublime Retreats PR department in Houston, she shook her head and sighed. Another bloody VIP trip. She loathed them with a passion. They were always demanding B list celebrities who never said thank you or tipped. She knew her job was much coveted amongst her friends, but they really didn't understand how taxing being a concierge for these high end guests was. It wasn't that she didn't enjoy working for SR, but she was ready for a break from it all. The final flight departure day couldn't come soon enough.

Never mind, just over a week to go and the season would be over and she could claim her life back again.

She carefully read through the details of the email, not recognising the lead name and arching an eyebrow slightly at the choice of villa. Seaview Cottage, although her personal favourite, was extremely remote, set halfway up a mountain in beautiful grounds with incredible views across to the sea, but it was a long way from the nearest town. Usually these 'types' liked to be seen and in the midst of what little action the tiny island had to offer, not locked away like hermits. She hoped this new guest realised he couldn't just stroll into town for dinner or whatever high jinks he had in mind and he would be happy with the location.

Not knowing the star in question, she Googled him but was none the wiser after looking through the first results. She'd left the UK years before and wasn't in the loop of what passed as popular culture these days and had no wish to be. She clicked on the images tab to see if a photograph would jog her memory and was inundated with pictures of a snarling, scrawny, blonde-haired man, most of which seemed to be related tabloid headlines of the worst kind.

"Fierce gets fiercer"

"Fierce throws up in Uber"

"Lupines in messy divorce"

Dear oh dear, he did not sound like a nice person at all, although by the notes on the booking he was bringing his sons with him so maybe he would be more amenable on holiday. "God, I would hate to be the centre of that much attention" she thought, as she read on through his Wiki page, trying to glean more information that would help her understand her guest and his needs, but all she discovered was that they were the same age and he was a Gemini.

Leonard John Lupine (born 20 June 1978) is an English actor, best known for his leading role as irascible DI Desmond Fierce in the British TV drama series Fierce Conflicts from 2008 to 2019.

It seemed all else he was famous for, apart from being rude, arrogant, antagonistic and an alcoholic, was marrying and then divorcing the petite pop star she vaguely recognised, Rennie Kenney, in an acrimonious affair that had kept the papers in business for quite some time. Looking through the pictures, she clicked on the only one where he could be seen smiling. It was a shot of him outside an excessive looking house holding his newly born son in his arms. His whole face lit up with joy, he actually looked extremely attractive when he smiled; it was a shame he didn't do it more often.

Well, he had better bloody behave himself here on Brač, I will not be pandering to any of that nonsense and neither will the locals she thought, crinkling her nose up as she pulled out her diary from the precious, multi coloured, brocade bag that she'd picked up in India, to enter his details on the appropriate page.

☼

Back in his 'Pied-à-terre' as the news hounds insisted on calling the tiny apartment he'd rented in haste after being thrown out of the marital home, Leonard was absently smiling to himself. With Mendelssohn playing in the background and feather duster in hand, he was working his way through his home, cleaning every inch of the place in a manner that would leave his TV fans quite frankly astounded.

His character, DI Fierce, was not just 'irascible' but dreadful in all aspects. He was rude to his colleagues and random people alike, he dropped litter, kicked dogs, ate takeaway straight from the foil containers and left them to develop mould. His day started and ended in a foul mood and there was no room for variation in-between. The only reason he kept his job on the force was his brilliant, Holmes like mind that always, of course, got his man or woman as the case may be.

It had been Angelica's shrewd idea, all those years ago when he first got the part, to carry his onscreen persona over to real life. She reasoned that the public would identify with him more strongly if on screen and off screen characters merged, and she was right. The series had taken off on its first run and his appalling behaviour at clubs and restaurants kept him constantly newsworthy; the country loved to hate him and couldn't get enough of his antics and millions tuned in every week to see how foul Fierce would be on his next adventure. He was the topic of conversation household-wide Saturday mornings after the show's previous night's airing on prime-time TV.

Over a decade later, and he was exhausted from playing the character. It was second nature now. He slipped on his raincoat and DI Fierce at the same time, but he was so firmly typecast in the TV role and in real life that he couldn't move on. He felt completely stuck. His only break from it all was behind closed doors with his guitar, creating his music or when his two boys were allowed to come and stay with him, which wasn't often enough as far as he was concerned.

When it came to the divorce, Rennie had taken his terrible personae and waved it in his face across a crowded courtroom, claiming sole rights to the children and limited access for himself and he'd felt helpless to argue the case with reams of media coverage to back her up and his recent unsuccessful rehab exploits still making headlines on a daily basis.

As the last strains of the music faded away, he finished polishing the leather sofa with a flourish and sank gratefully onto it, flicking on the curved screen TV with the remote as he did so. Unfortunately, the first thing he saw was a closeup of his loathed ex-wife, standing outside his ex-home giving a statement to the press. As he turned up the volume, he heard:

'Whirlwind romance?' as a reporter finished asking a question. Rennie gave her trademark Betty Boop giggle and expertly tossed her mane of blonde extensions.

'Yes, it has been rather sudden, but the best things are, aren't they?' she trilled sickeningly, causing Leonard to flinch in a Pavlovian reaction to the sound which grated on him like fingernails down a blackboard.

'Show us the ring' a voice called out and, making a jolly good job of looking shy, she hesitantly displayed her left hand, now bearing the most enormous diamond he'd ever seen. He sat up, shocked, and watched the rest of the news segment describing the romance between Rennie and John Elvers, the latest onscreen heartthrob from a reality TV show that was currently top pick for the viewing public. As the news announcer declared that the couple were planning to get married in an undisclosed location next week, Leonard jumped up, cursing loudly in true DI Fierce fashion.

No wonder that conniving bitch agreed he could have the kids next week; she was planning a romantic escape with that nitwit and didn't want them under her feet! Reaching automatically for the whiskey bottle, he poured a large measure and drank it down straight with a trembling hand. Little did the public know that her cute little girl next door persona was a complete fiction. Underneath those batting eyelashes was a wildcat with vicious tendencies and everything she did was premeditated, poisonous, and self-obsessed.

They had been brought together by Angelica, who saw their match as an agent's dream promotion wise and he'd endured six years of hell with her before making his escape. But only after he'd agreed that she was going to be the victim in this scenario as far as the world and the press was concerned and he would have to take the blame for everything, which he agreed to readily in his desperation to be off the leash.

And now here she was with some other poor, helpless sap in tow. Well, good luck to him, he was going to need it. As he reached for the bottle to pour another drink, he stopped himself; a car was picking him up early tomorrow morning to take him to the studio first thing to film the final episode of this series and he wanted it to go smoothly.

He knew all too well from experience, turning up hung-over did not help the proceedings and was a painful process for him and everyone else concerned with the production. He put the bottle away and picked up his guitar instead; strumming it until he felt calmer and losing himself in the sweet melody, he tried to finish the song he was currently trying to write.

It was a plaintive love ballad, describing unrequited love, but he couldn't quite find the words to finish it. He wasn't even sure what had inspired him, but it had just started to flow naturally from his pen one day and he knew in his heart of hearts it was good. He just longed to find the missing words to complete it. He had tried so many times but the words just weren't there, he needed some kind of inspiration.

Maybe it was because he had always been so unlucky in love that the words wouldn't flow. He always felt so content when he could just sit and write and play his guitar. The creative process soothed him in a way nothing else did, and he longed for a time when he could just do that and nothing else. His ideal world consisted of his boys, and a private studio somewhere remote and possibly someone to share it with, although he found that hard to imagine.

An email pinged through from Angelica, disturbing his reverie, confirming the arrangements for his holiday, including flights, car hire and villa details for two days' time. It seemed to be very swiftly organised, but she had always been a Pitbull for details, that's what made her good at her job. She might drive him crazy with her machinations, but she was a damn good agent.

This reminded him, his new contract had arrived by courier this morning. He looked over to where it sat, demanding attention on the counter. The thought of signing it made him feel physically sick, so he ignored it, and looked at his upcoming destination instead.

The island of Brač in Croatia, he'd never heard of it, so looked it up, wanting to see that it would provide a suitable getaway for him and the boys. It seemed remote enough for his purposes and the villa looked stunning, it had a heated pool, the boys would certainly love that. He was warming to this idea the more he thought about it. A week in Croatia away from the press, his public, his agent, it sounded like heaven.

The fact that Alex and Ben would be there was the icing on the cake. He loved his sons ferociously, they were the only reason he'd lasted six years with his god-awful wife. If all this week was going to cost him was a couple of artsy pics for this company to claim bragging rights, then where was the harm? Another email popped up as he was looking at delightful sunny harbours full of small colourful boats and happy looking, tanned holidaymakers enjoying everything the tiny island had to offer.

From: Isabella.angelo@sublimeretreats.com
To: ljl@yahoo.co.uk
Subject: Sea View Cottage

Dear Mr Lupine,

Hello and dobro jutro (Good Morning)

Your Sublime Retreats Villas experience is fast approaching and I am emailing you on behalf of the company to begin working on your vacation itinerary. I look forward to planning all the activities you wish to enjoy while in Brač.

My name is Isabella Angelo and I am your Local Concierge based on Brač near your Villa.

My role is to work with you and to answer any questions you have and help you to build your Croatian itinerary. From now until your arrival at the villa, I am your point of contact for your Croatian retreat, so please direct your questions to me and I will get back to you right away. Upon arrival at the villa in Brač, I will meet you and introduce you to the villa and ensure everything is organized so that you can enjoy the vacation of a lifetime.

What I need from you: The first steps in planning an exceptional trip are to ensure you have provided us with your guest list, arrival information and your grocery requests. Please reply to this email with a list of your guests and their approximate ages. I have included a grocery list for you to fill out, so your villa will be stocked prior to your arrival.

Activities: We have designed a suggested "Sublime Week" itinerary for your stay to highlight a few of the exciting activities that are available, please find attached. Use it as a starting point to discuss your itinerary with me. I look forward to hearing back from you and planning your wonderful vacation on Brač Island.

Regards,
Isabella Angelo
Sublime Retreats Concierge

From:ljl@yahoo.co.uk
To: Isabella.angelo@sublimeretreats.com
Subject: Sea View Cottage

Dear Isabella,
Thank you so much for your email.
No guests as such, just my two boys; Ben who is 5 and Alexander who is 7 going on 45!
I believe the company wants us to try some of the local activities; I think the horse riding would be great for us and I guess we could try the local chef?
If that's ok?
I don't want to do too much, just relax and enjoy time with my boys.

Many Thanks,

Leonard

Isabella was taken aback by the tone of his email. He didn't sound at all mean and nasty as she'd been expecting. No abrupt list of demands, just this rather timid and extremely polite missive. Maybe this week wouldn't be so tough after all despite her concerns, but she knew better than to try and second guess her guests' personalities from their emails. She'd fallen foul of that before and mentally braced herself to be ready for anything.

Twisting her wayward hair into a bun and stabbing a pen in to secure it, she rang the maid of the villa to let her know they had a last-minute booking and sent out some emails to try and find a chef. This time of year, most of her regular cooks had left the island for their winter jobs elsewhere and it would be a hard task to find someone at this stage.

Aware that time was getting away from her; she popped her phone into her pocket and walked out into the brilliant sunshine that was bathing the small garden that surrounded her house. This was her happy place, where she felt most relaxed and centred. She spent hours out here tending the flowers and her vegetable plot, which she'd planted with all her favourite herbs as well as enough tomatoes, courgettes and aubergines to feed her and Luka all year round.

She had got her green fingers from her father; he had been obsessed with growing everything he could his entire life. Some of her happiest memories of her dad were with him in their enormous garden in Yorkshire, following him around with a miniature wheelbarrow and flower covered wellington boots and 'helping' him plant and weed. She remembered sitting on the workbench in his potting shed, watching him gently transplant seedlings and mix up his magic formula for potting soil, the secret for which he had passed onto her before he died.

Standing up stiffly after pulling up the latest batch of persistent weeds that had appeared around her prized plants she checked the time on her phone and realised she needed to get a wriggle on if she was going to have time to shower before meeting her friend Sandy for a coffee.

6am on a cold morning is not a good time to be up in London, Leonard decided as he stared out the window at grey streets. Sipping his strong, black coffee from his reusable cup in the back of the car that had picked him up, he tried to ignore the chatty driver, who was far too perky for his liking. His grumpy persona came in useful sometimes, and after a couple of grunts, the driver got the hint and gave up and the drive continued in blissful silence.

Watching the damp, drab streets slide by the sun-lit, colourful images he'd been looking at last night of his holiday destination popped into his head and his mood improved immediately. He was long overdue a break, whatever Angelica's purpose behind this trip, and he knew her well enough to know there was one, and he was infused with a sense of adventure at the prospect of getting away from the monotone of what passed as his current life.

Pulling smoothly into the studio lot, the car was waved through and as he got out, an assistant ran over with another coffee ready for him in one hand and today's script to take into make up with him in the other. Reading through the pages, he was unsurprised to see that DC Fierce was left hanging over a cliff in the final scene. It was the usual hook, a literal cliff-hanger.

'John.' He called to the director as he walked through the makeup area 'I've been thinking. Maybe it's time to give Desmond a hidden talent? '

'We are not having you playing a guitar,' grumbled John wearily with the air of one much put upon 'I am tired of having this conversation with you, Leonard, it just doesn't fit. There's no way DC Fierce is going to come over all lyrical after ten bloody years, is there?

'Well, he could. It could be a childhood hobby he takes up again,' Leonard pouted.

Shaking his head, John patted his shoulder, 'not this season Leonard, now, let's get this show on the road.'

Pulling the tissue from around his neckline, Leonard stood up and slouched into Studio 2, where the first scenes were being filmed: DI Fierce's revolting apartment. God, he detested this place. He felt itchy every time he came in here, the sooner this was finished the better. Thinking ahead to seeing his boys and spending a whole week with them in a wonderful, new place, an uncharacteristic smile spread across his face.

'Take that silly grin off your face,' barked John. 'You're about to discuss the dreadful discovery of a dismembered body which is nothing to grin about!'

Snapping back to attention, Leonard took his place for the scene and waited for the director to call 'action'.

Isabella, looking up from her phone and her idle online browsing for Diptyque candles, smiled as her friend Sandy pulled up a chair beside her at their favourite café on the harbour front in Bol. The tightly packed tables and chairs, shaded by the large umbrellas touting ice creams, on the sandstone promenade that edged the sea was the perfect spot to while away the hours with girly chat and friendship.

Rising to greet her and kissing her on both cheeks, she was happy to see her. They'd become firm friends when Isabella spent her first summer on the island, working at the restaurant that Sandy ran with her ex-husband. Their initial bond of being two northern lasses was reinforced by being single women in a foreign country, and they both had come to rely on the support that this provided.

Isabella had been surprised one night, over the inevitable after work glass of wine, when Sandy revealed to her the reason for her divorce. She blithely divulged that her Josip was gay. And as much as they genuinely loved each other, he finally, after several years of marriage, felt he had to come clean, despite his family's horror. Much to everyone's amazement, the couple had remained firm friends and continued to work happily together at the restaurant, things actually running more smoothly with the relationship on its new footing.

'How are things with you?' Sandy asked, pushing her blonde hair behind her ear as she beckoned to the waiter 'Phew it's cracking flags today. What's with this weather? Are you ready for the end of season?'

'Well I was, but I've had another bloody booking through. One of those infernal "influencers" is coming for a week and I have to entertain him!'

Sandy laughed, knowing all too well her friend's distaste for the so called famous guests who had to be treated with kid gloves and, after ordering her coffee, asked

'Which lucky star has the pleasure of your company this time, anyone I'd know?'

'I doubt it' observed Isabella dismissively 'hang on a minute, it was Leonard something' she added, reaching into her bag and then flipping through her diary until she came to the right page, 'Ah, here it is, Leonard Lupine, apparently he's in some TV show.'

Sandy squealed loudly, causing customers nearby to glance round. 'You are joking. Leonard Lupine is coming here? Oh my God, that's belting that I love that guy, and he is super-hot! All brooding and sultry, are you seriously telling me you don't know who he is?'

Isabella was a little taken aback; she would never

have pegged Sandy for a groupie. 'Settle down. It's not such a big deal, so some mardy TV bloke is coming here, and I wouldn't call him hot, let alone super-hot!' she laughed, taking a sip of her cappuccino.

Sandy shook her head in disbelief at her friend's blasé attitude to what she found exhilarating news; she gave a mental shake and tried to rein in her elation a little, and attempted to get onto Isabella's level.

'OK, Isabella, what you have to understand, despite the little bubble you insist on living in, is that the rest of the world pays attention to what is going on, especially on TV. Your upcoming guest has been headline news for 10 years or so, and like him or not you cannot ignore the fact that if he doesn't enjoy his stay here, it will have a huge impact on the company you work for and probably the island as a whole. If he slags off Brač, then it will definitely put people off visiting. Do you want that on your conscience?'

'I always make sure my guests have a fantastic time,' bleated Isabella, flushing and looking slightly offended. 'I don't care who they are, I treat them all equally!'

'I just think you should pull out even more stops out for this one, that's all,' said Sandy mollifyingly, 'and also let your lovely friend know where to find him when he decides to eat out. She might want the chance to chat up the poor lonely man and make his holiday even more special' she snickered with a sly wink that made Isabella laugh.

'I solemnly swear to be on my best behaviour, which includes' she declared sternly, pointing a finger at her with an angry timpani of bangles descending 'not divulging my guest's itinerary! Although if you fancy a spot of cooking, I am in desperate need of a chef, I can't find one for love nor money at this time of year.'

Sandy spluttered out some coffee. Dabbing her chin with a napkin, she looked startled 'You know fine well I'm no cook, I even burn pasta. I'm not like you, all Nigella in the kitchen.' She paused, mid sip, looking thoughtful for a moment before a mischievous twinkle appeared in her eyes.

'That's it! You should cook for him! It's the quickest way to a man's heart and God knows it's about time you had a man,' she beamed, clapping gleefully at her cunning plan. 'You can impress him with your gastronomy and he can repay you with an orgasm!' and she burst into peals of laughter.

Isabella couldn't help smiling even as she shook her head at her friend. Sandy's eternal efforts to find her a fella were trying at times, but she had to admit it did make her laugh.

'You know full well Sandy that I have no interest in men.'

'Don't give me that rot. You just feel like you have to behave like mother Teresa because Luka's dad died before he was born. It's about time you jumped out of those dismal widow's weeds and started to live again. It's been four years, Isabella.'

Taken aback, Isabella looked out across the bay where the small fishing boats bobbed in unison, unsure how to respond. Her friend was right, of course.

Even now, here in company, the loneliness was there. Flitting around the edges of her thoughts and waiting to erupt as soon as she got home, the weight of being stuck here on the island that was Luka's heritage was oppressive sometimes.

Crossing her legs and fixing her large green eyes on Sandy as she came back to reality, she mused, 'you may have an idea there. Not...' she snapped, raising a finger again, to stop the flow of chatter about to spew forth from her excitable friend '... Not about the man, but the cooking. I can easily rustle something up for this Leonard and his boys and let's face it, a bit of extra cash towards the winter is always handy.'

Knowing when to leave well alone, Sandy remarked, 'you're right, a bit of extra cash will be good, and after all, what harm can it do?'

Sinking back into the leather seat of the car that was threading its way through the rush hour traffic to take him home, Leonard finally allowed himself to have a drink from the built-in bar. Letting out a heartfelt sigh as the tension left his body; he closed his eyes and began to mentally pack his suitcase.

Tomorrow afternoon, his driver would bring his boys, and they could head to the airport. Their flight was very early the following morning, so Angelica had booked them into the Sofitel at Gatwick for the night. Butterflies started to mount as he drained his glass just as they pulled up outside his home; he was really looking forward to this.

He ran the usual gauntlet of press hounds, rapidly firing questions at him about Rennie's engagement, all of which he ignored with a scowl, before flinging himself into the sanctuary of his hallway. Happily shrugging off his trench coat for what he hoped would be the last time for a long while, he began to hum as he went to retrieve his dusty suitcase from the top of the wardrobe.

From: Isabella.angelo@sublimeretreats.com
To: ljl@yahoo.co.uk
Subject: Sea View Cottage

Dear Mr. Lupine,

I hope you are well and looking forward to your trip!

Please find attached a sample menu for you to choose from for your private chef experience.

If you could let me know which dishes you would like for each course at your earliest convenience, it will allow the chef time to prepare your gourmet experience.

With regards to horse riding, which day would you like to go? If you let me know, I can check availability and get you booked in.

Also, please find attached the driving instructions, which will guide you once you arrive on the ferry at Supatar, to the villa by the simplest route.

If you have any questions or have other activities, you would like booked please don't hesitate to email me. I can recommend the day trip to Hvar; it's a wonderful place and well worth a visit.

Best regards,

Isabella Angelo
Sublime Retreats Concierge

From:ljl@yahoo.co.uk
To: Isabella.angelo@sublimeretreats.com
Subject: Sea View Cottage

Good Afternoon Isabella,

Many thanks for your email. With regards to the chef meal, is it possible to just have something simple such as fried chicken fillets with some vegetables for the main course? Although all the meals look exquisite on the menu, my boys have very simple tastes and I fear it would be a wasted effort on the cooks' part to make anything more complicated. No need for starters and a selection of the local desserts would be perfect!

Horse riding, I think we should do a few days into the trip, after the excitement of the pool starts to wear off! I'll leave it to you to book a suitable time.

And yes, please to the trip to Hvar. I've had a quick look, and it looks lovely, I think the boys would enjoy it.
Thank you so much for all your help.

Best wishes,
Leonard

Isabella had just pulled up outside Luka's grandparents' house to pick him up on her way home when the email arrived. Quickly reading through it as she got out of her car and made her way towards the tiny, old stone cottage where they lived just outside Murvica, she was struck once again by the polite, almost meek tone of the email. It seemed greatly at odds with everything she had read about the man, and something didn't seem to ring true. Jekyll and Hyde sprang to mind, and she fervently hoped it was Dr. Jekyll who would be arriving on the island on Saturday.

Hearing the familiar shriek of welcome from her son she looked up to see him barrelling towards her with his usual gusto and, all thoughts of TV stars forgotten, she crouched down; arms open wide to receive the inevitable bear hug.

'Mum, mum, I saw a beetle, it was huuuuge!' Luka spouted 'Grandma said not to worry about it but I ran away anyway, it was a bit too buzzy for me!' he announced before burying himself in her arms. Feeling the usual burst of love that her boy stirred in her, she laughed and breathed in his familiar soapy scent, which acted as a panacea to any errant negative emotions she had.

'Isy, come on in and have something to drink before you drive home,' called Ana, Luka's Grandma from the arched doorway where she was watching them with a smile. Nodding in consent, she swept the boy up in her arms and walked into their comfortable kitchen to catch up with Ana and her husband, Ivan.

She had met Luka's dad when she'd set out on her backpacking tour that was set to take her around the world over five years ago. Her trip to India in the year before had created a wanderlust in her that couldn't be ignored. Croatia had been her first stop and meeting Mateo had delayed her journey for 6 weeks before she could drag herself away. She knew he was heartbroken, but she also knew that if she didn't carry on her journey, it would never happen.

Promising herself and Mateo that she would return, she took the ferry to Split and the airport to fly to Athens. She spent a wonderful three days there exploring the ancient monuments before catching the ferry to Chios; even though she missed Mateo dreadfully, her sense of adventure propelled her onwards.

Two weeks later, in the toilets of a tiny café in a village on Limnos, she sat staring at the little blue line on the white stick that was telling her that her life was about to change. Fate had played her cards and Isabella didn't think twice about travelling back to Croatia as quickly as she could to the loving arms of the father of her baby.

Her excitement mounting as the ferry slipped into Supatar, she couldn't wait to see the look on Mateo's face when he saw her and she told him the news. Unfortunately, fate had other plans and when she arrived at the family house, she learned the shocking news that her wonderful Mateo had been cruelly snatched from them in a car accident only days before.

She spent three days sobbing her heart out in her hotel bedroom before pulling herself together. Right, she thought, I am obviously destined to be here, so I had better make the most of it. When she finally told Mateo's parents that she was expecting their grandchild, the tears of joy were overwhelming. It would never make up for the loss of their son, but to know a little piece of him was still here went a long way towards healing their broken hearts.

They welcomed her into the family with open arms, and although she decided to find her own home, rather than take up their offer of staying with them, she didn't hesitate to involve them in Luka's life and was thankful for their unerring support which meant she could actually work and make a life for them both. Ana and Ivan were always happy to have their grandson, day or night, and were eternally grateful to Isabella for choosing to stay on the island, which in some ways made her feel a little trapped.

She loved Brač, and she enjoyed her life there, but she still yearned to finish the journey she started all those years ago, even though she knew she could never take Luka away from his home.

HOLIDAY

I t was a typical grey, drizzly London day when the car picked up Leonard to take him to the airport, but the beaming faces of his sons in the back seat eclipsed any gloomy thoughts and their enthusiasm for the adventure ahead was infectious. As they motored towards Gatwick, he tried to keep up with their never-ending stream of questions and observations, feeling quite worn out by the time they reached the hotel. Their joy when he produced two disposable cameras for them to use, to keep a record of their holidays, far exceeded their cost.

'Ok boys, use them wisely, and don't use all the film up all in one day. Keep them safe in your bags; you're both in charge of your backpacks.' He smiled fondly as both boys carefully and proudly put the cameras in their bags. He was so thrilled to finally be able to spend real time with them; the odd weekend really wasn't enough. He would have to try and negotiate again with Renee when he got back. Maybe her newly married bliss would make her a little more amenable to his request.

The young receptionist simpered and fluttered her extended eyelashes at him all the way through the check in procedure but Leonard ignored her, only rewarding her with a brief smile when she mentioned that she had upgraded him to a Superior queen with runway view. Taking the proffered key card without a word, he herded the boys towards the bank of lifts, trying to keep them focused on getting up to the room, whilst the receptionist treated his retreating back to a look that should have burnt his shirt off.

The couple already standing in the lift did a double take when he stepped in and when he went to press the button for his floor, the man immediately stepped forward and said in revered tones, 'let me get that sir, which floor?'

Hesitating before replying, you never know what people might do with such information; Leonard eventually decided he looked harmless enough and tried to maintain his smile as they bombarded him with questions before finally getting out two floors below his.

Entering the room, the boys were ecstatic, bouncing straight across the beds to the window, which gave a perfect view of the constant stream of aircraft arriving and departing and would obviously keep them mesmerised for the whole evening.

'Can we stay here all week, Dad?' asked Ben, nose stuck to the window, admiring the circling formation of planes' banking, awaiting their turn to land.

'I'm afraid not, Benny, we're getting on one of those planes tomorrow and heading for a wonderful place called Brač.'

'But I wanna stay here' the small boy pouted, smearing the glass, still unable to drag his eyes away from the spectacle on the other side of the window and looking very much like his father.

Not wanting a full scale melt down on his hands, Leonard went over, knelt down and gave his son's skinny frame a hug.

'Why don't you take a couple of pictures with your new camera?' he asked 'that way you can look at this view forever.'

Pulling away eagerly, Ben ran around the room. 'Dad, Dad, where's my bag, Dad? Where did you put my backpack?'

Glancing round distractedly, Leonard queried, 'where did you leave it Benny? You are in charge of your bag, you know that.'

A frantic, if brief, search only highlighted its absence and Benny burst into tears 'My camera' he wailed. 'My iPad! Mr Kernuffel!' and he threw himself face down on the bed and began to sob his heart out.

Dreading the loss of the much loved, never left behind, and impossible to sleep without, battered old rag that his son called Mr. Kernuffle more than anything else that might be in the bag, his mind raced. He definitely remembered helping Ben put it on his back as they got the luggage out of the boot of the car, so it must be here somewhere. Racing to the door and wrenching it open, he called back, 'Alex, you're in charge. Do not leave this room or answer the door to anyone. I won't be five minutes.'

Closing the door firmly behind him, he ran to the lifts, tapping his fingers against his thigh until one of them opened, leapt in and stabbed at the button repeatedly until the doors finally shut and it started to descend. The journey down was interminable; his brain couldn't even begin to cope with the consequences if he didn't find this bloody toy. A week of tears and no sleep, for starters. The boy would probably refuse to get on the plane, let alone anything else. It was an intolerable thought.

Forcing the doors to open on the ground floor, he ran over to the reception and waited impatiently for the woman he'd seen earlier to finish checking in the family there. Summoning a smile as he approached the now slightly frosty looking receptionist, 'I don't suppose someone has found a small backpack,' he mumbled apologetically, 'it's blue, with small planes dotted all over it. It's my son's, he left it somewhere' he rambled under her icy stare.

Slowly reaching down, she plucked up the errant bag and held it aloft triumphantly. 'Would this be what you are looking for, "Detective"?' she asked, smirking in a way that made him want to slap her. But with relief flooding through his entire body and visibly radiating off him, he couldn't help but smile.

'Oh my God, thank you so much! I have no idea what we would have done if you hadn't found it. You're an angel!' he exclaimed, causing her to blush and replace her frosty manner with a simper as she handed it over.

Loping bank to the lift, feeling so much lighter, he pressed the button for his floor and hummed happily, hugging the bag to his chest, as the lift slid upwards. It stopped at level 5 and then started to descend again. Puzzled, he shook his head and narrowed his eyes. "Someone must have called it back down," he thought. But when the doors slid open on the ground floor, there was nobody standing there. He could see the receptionist looking at him strangely, so he jabbed the button for his floor again. This time when the lift stopped at the 5th floor he started to panic; his boys were alone in the room, he had to get back.

Looking around, he finally registered the notices pinned all around the lift stating that only guests staying at the hotel in possession of a room key could travel beyond the 5th floor. With wide eyes and a sinking feeling, he began to hopelessly pat his pockets, but he knew he didn't have it with him; he'd thrown it on the desk as soon as they'd gone in the room.

"Oh my God, I can't believe I have been so stupid!" he thought, blanching at the thought of having to face that receptionist again as the lift began its descent once more and he imagined the headlines shouting about the famous detective who couldn't even navigate to his hotel room. Angelica would have a fit and no mistake and he really couldn't blame her. Steeling himself for a charm offensive as the doors slid open, he stood back to let in an older lady who was smiling at him with the familiar look of recognition that he usually dreaded.

'Ooh, are you staying here too?' she exclaimed 'my word, my daughter will never believe I have been in a lift with Leonard Lupine' she prattled on, airily waving her key card at the sensor and pressing the button for the floor below his. Quickly pressing for his floor, he sagged with relief and rewarded her with a smile, and let her excited chatter wash over him until she reached her floor.

When he finally, thankfully, walked up to his door, he gave a sharp rap to announce his presence. There was silence from the other side.

'Alex, Ben, it's me, Dad' he called. The silence continued, but then he heard a shuffling noise and whispering.

'How do we know it's you?' Called Alex.

'Come on, don't muck about, you can hear it's me.'

'But you said not to open the door to anyone,' called Ben in an unusual moment of clarity for the small boy.

Frowning, Leonard thought for a minute, then, rummaging through the back pack pulled out the rather soiled and tattered remnants of Mr Kernuffle.

'I think you can open the door to Mr Kernuffle no matter what I said, don't you?'

As he'd expected, the door was flung open and Ben snatched the toy from him, holding it to his chest for dear life, his small face beatific with joy.

Shutting the door thankfully behind him, he went straight to the minibar, determined to reward himself for surviving the close shave and publicity nightmare. But the cupboard was bare. Damn and blast Angelica. She knew him too well. Getting the staff in hotels to remove temptation was an old trick of hers, but he was on holiday damn it!

Looking at his watch and making sure to grab his key card this time 'Right boys,' he called, 'I think it's dinnertime, don't you?' She can't have emptied the entire restaurant of alcohol, he thought fervently as, after double checking both boys had their bags, he marched determinedly out the door.

Standing on the terrace of Sea View Cottage soaking in the morning sun, Isabella took a deep, cleansing breath and murmured her affirmations. She liked to start each day with a positive attitude and welcome everything that the universe had to offer with an open heart and mind. Once she felt calm and centred, she pulled out the checklist she'd prepared so she could go around the villa with a fine-tooth comb and make sure everything was just right.

Mia, the maid, was just finishing up so, carefully avoiding the wet floors, she started her inspection. She loved this house, the shabby chic décor with its modern touches; the sanded wooden floors and white furniture offset with splashes of cerise were exactly how she would eventually like her house to look. The terraces, with views across to the neighbouring island of Hvar, were stunning and she could quite happily sit there all day, given the chance.

Sometimes, when the villa was empty, which wasn't often, she would sneak up there with her book and some wine and have a blissful afternoon there, pretending it was hers. She had heard on the gossip grapevine that the English owners were planning to sell it, and she idly daydreamed about winning the lottery so she could make it her own. She couldn't imagine a more perfect spot to bring up her son and she imagined a life there with a fictitious husband and the possibility of another child, a girl this time, as she made her way around the house, double checking everything would be perfect for her incoming guests.

She checked that the Wi-Fi was working, tested the TV and the Bluetooth speaker and laid out Sublime Retreats notepads and pens at various spots around the villa as she checked off all the quality points on her list with the satisfaction of a job well done.

☼

As the plane started its descent into Split airport, both boys were glued to the small window, exclaiming with joy at everything they could see. The flight had made good time and Leonard calculated that they would have an hour or so spare to stop in the city for lunch before getting the afternoon ferry to Brač.

The luggage came through unexpectedly quickly and, ignoring the whispers and glances of the crowd around the luggage belt as people began to realise who he was, he shouldered his backpack, efficiently pulled out the handles of the cases and started to wheel them it towards the exit, calling for the boys to keep up and not get lost.

At the car hire desk, he was thankfully greeted by blank faces. Obviously, DI Fierce had made little impact here, he was happy to see. After signing the necessary paperwork, one of the rental staff walked them across the road to the parking area and stopped by a bright, metallic green Opal which, to the boys' delight, was called Karl. Cramming their bags in the boot before getting the boys strapped in, Leonard let out a sigh of relief as he slid into the driver's seat.

He suddenly realised it had been a long, long time since he had been in this position, actually in charge of where he was heading, with no appointments to rule him, and he felt a great sense of freedom. After checking he knew where all the controls were and adjusting the mirrors, he flicked on the radio and found a local station playing current pop music.

'Right boys, adventure awaits. Let's go find some food!' he declared and, slipping the car easily into gear, edged out onto the main road and followed the signs for Split.

The road got busier as they neared the main part of the town. Traffic flowed alarmingly and horns blared as Leonard hesitated, unsure of where to go. He had planned to park near the port area but, as he was shunted along that road with the press of the traffic, there didn't seem to be any available spaces and he found the car being sucked back with the flow towards the centre.

Spotting a likely looking space, he zipped in. Looking around at the other cars parked along the road seemed to confirm it was ok to be here and there were no meters in sight, so he happily unloaded the boys and they walked back down to the waterfront in search of some burgers. It didn't take long to find a suitable, gaudy looking burger joint, and they happily dived in and found a table. Leonard wasn't much of a one for fast food but, knowing his poor kids always ended up on whatever faddy diet Rennie was on at the time, he tried to indulge them when he could.

As they swallowed the last mouthfuls of what turned out to be delicious homemade burgers, Leonard checked the time. The ferry was in an hour which gave them plenty of time to get to the port just down the road but he wanted to get there early to work out where to go. He hated being stressed about travelling, so always left plenty of time. After paying the bill, they gathered their bags and walked slowly back to the car, admiring the buildings and shop fronts along the way.

Walking into the square where he'd parked the car, Leonard's confident stride faltered as he became aware of a certain lack of shiny green car in the spot he thought it should be. In fact, there was an entirely different, un-Karl like vehicle casually occupying the space. Spinning around comically, frantically searching to confirm the landmarks he'd noted as they'd left and wildly hoping to see a flash of green somewhere in the vicinity, his heart sank.

'Where's Karl?' piped up Alex, looking around. 'Has someone stolen him?' he whispered, eyes darting and clutching his bag securely to his chest in case said thieves were still lurking somewhere unseen.

'Umm' Leonard responded distractedly, mind racing with the possible knock-on effects of whatever had happened to the bloody car, 'I'm sure it's nothing to worry about' he asserted crouching down to their level, trying to reassure their concerned little faces. 'Daddy just needs a moment to think'.

As he looked around helplessly, he became aware of a uniformed figure walking slowly along the street towards him, clipboard in hand, carefully studying all of the cars as he passed. Suddenly he stopped and smirked and with a practiced motion, lifted the walkie talkie clipped to his jacket to his mouth and let out a stream of words Leonard could only assume meant 'we've got another one!' Sure enough, within minutes, a large tow truck came barrelling around the corner and pulled up efficiently alongside the offending vehicle. The driver leapt out and started the routine of strapping the wheels to the lifting equipment on his truck.

'Wait there boys,' called Leonard and jogged over to the two men. 'Excuse me, my car has been taken, do you know where it is?'

The men looked at him blankly for a moment, and then the truck driver stammered 'no speak English' with a shrug and a look that implied he was extremely remorseful about his lack of linguistics. Looking helpless for a second, Leonard suddenly pulled the car keys out of his pocket and waved them in the faces of the slightly alarmed looking men. He pointed to the space where the car had been and then pantomimed looking for it. Realisation dawned on their faces and the driver took the keys from him and looked at the fob which had the details on it.

Another walkie talkie conversation ensued, followed by a beaming smile which Leonard took to mean they'd found it. Pulling a scrap of paper from the dash of his truck, the driver wrote down the address of the car pound where Karl was being held to ransom. Taking the slip of paper gratefully, Leonard mimed his heartfelt thanks as best he could then, looking about him, questioned hopefully 'taxi?'

'tamo gore' gushed the first man, pointing up the busy road leading off the square and holding up five fingers, presumably to indicate how many minutes it would take, Leonard hoped, rather than the miles involved. Once again thanking them profusely and making a mental note to at least learn some basic words of Croatian this week, he swept up the boys in his wake as he trotted in the direction of salvation.

Fifteen frantic minutes later, he finally spotted and hailed a taxi. Thrusting the boys in the back seat, he jumped in the front and showed the driver the scrap of paper with the address on it.

'Ah, you parked wrong,' laughed the driver with a smirk on his face as he pulled out wildly into the constant stream of traffic to a deafening round of horn blowing. 'You are here for holiday?' he asked, glancing at Leonard and doing a comical double take. 'Oh, my' he crowed with his eyes still firmly on his passenger, 'DI Fierce is in my taxi!!'

'Yes, yes' shouted Leonard jabbing a finger at the road, causing the driver to refocus and swerve the taxi just in time to avoid a bus paused at the traffic lights, and go sailing gaily across the junction apparently oblivious to the red light and cacophony of horns yet again.

'I am Jakov and I am number one fan of Fierce Conflicts. I watch them all many, many times,' stated the driver, casting adoring looks at Leonard, his bushy eyebrows waggling their enthusiasm.

'Well, if you can get us to the car pound in about 12 minutes so I have enough time to catch my ferry to Brač I will become the biggest fan of Jakov and you will earn yourself a huge tip' said Leonard with a grin as the car lurched forward with even less consideration for other road users than before. There were some advantages to being famous.

Sure enough, they arrived in ten minutes flat and Jakov took charge of the situation, shouting at the officious-looking clerk behind the counter and gesticulating wildly in Leonard's direction. After a brief exchange of heated debate, the clerk checked the licence details on the key fob and, muttering all the while, pulled out the paperwork and stamped it angrily before pushing it towards Leonard to sign. Once he had paid the fine, the clerk seemed to cheer up if not speed up. Pushing his glasses firmly into place, he sauntered towards the carpark to retrieve Karl.

'Bloody bastards' exploded Jakov suddenly, his expressive eyebrows in action again, 'give them a little power and they think they are God! I hates them I do Mr Lupine, hates them' he hissed emphatically.

'Call me Leonard and I know what you mean, but

never mind,' he began, glancing at his watch. 'I think I still have time even with his performance.'

'Don't you worry Mr Lupine, my brother, he works the boats, I call 'im now to tell him to wait' proclaimed Jakov happily, fishing his phone out of his snug-fitting jeans and clamping it to his ear.'

'Leonard, please, and there really is no...' he trailed off as Jakov started once again barking instructions, this time into his phone and presumably to his brother.

A short while later, Leonard carefully navigated Karl into the port, following Jakov, who had insisted on leading the way, and was able to drive straight onto the ferry that was indeed a few minutes past its due sailing time. As he stepped out of the car, Jakov materialised in front of him and enveloped him in a heartfelt bear hug.

'So good to meet yous, Mr Lupine,' he muttered, his eyes suspiciously bright and glassy. 'My family is from Brač. You need anything, anything at all while you are there you calls me OK?' he effused, pressing his business card into Leonard's unresisting hand. With a wave at a man in the distance who bore the same squat, broad-shouldered stamp and was undoubtedly his brother, he stomped off the boat with a dreamy smile on his rugged face. Leonard could just imagine the man's story telling later today about how he had met and helped the famous detective.

They made their way up the stairs to one of the outside seating areas as, with a clang of the huge door closing and the juddering of the hefty, rusted chain being winched up, the ancient ferry began its slow departure from the port. Choosing a spot in the sun where they could enjoy the scenery, the three of them sat in companionable silence, happy to be on the last leg of the journey and enjoying the exotic scenes and smells assailing them from all angles.

With a light breeze deflecting some of the unaccustomed heat and the unrecognisable, soporific chatter around him, Leonard felt almost dreamlike he was so relaxed. Stretching out his long legs with a contented sigh, he smiled at his sons who were discussing what photos to take and realised no matter what was missing from his life, here and now he was happy.

☼

Once she was sure everything was shipshape at the villa for the arrival of her 'star' later that afternoon, she drove down to her in-laws' house to pick up Luka and take him to their favourite beach, Zlatni Rat. During high season, she avoided it completely as it became far too busy for her liking, but in October it was idyllic and they spent as much time as they could there.

The long swathes of golden looking pebbles kept Luka entertained for hours before they both dived into the beautiful blue waters. He had her love for the sea and they were both at their happiest, diving in and jumping over waves. He'd even finally mastered the art of snorkeling, so, side by side, they explored the underworld together, before eventually flopping out onto the beach to dry out and deciding when they would come back.

After a relaxing afternoon with her son, Isabella drove them home where Sandy was waiting to entertain him whilst she got showered and put her uniform on to go up to the villa and wait to greet her guests. It was part of her role to be there to meet them and show them around the property when they arrived, pointing out all they needed to know so they could settle straight in.

'There's spaghetti Bolognese ready for dinner. Make sure he eats some, but I should be home in time to put him to bed,' she remarked as she walked into the lounge, towel drying her mass of curly brunette hair. She smiled at her friend, engrossed in the colouring book with Luka, squabbling over who would fill in which part.

'Take your time,' Sandy replied happily before adding with a smirk, 'spend as long as you like with the lovely Leonard. We'll be fine!'

'He should be there about 6.30 so I will be back about an hour after that unless he's particularly demanding' Isabella said, ignoring her friend's inferences and winding her hair up into a bun, skillfully stabbing it with a pen to secure it.

'Suit yourself. Just saying if you're having a nice time, don't hurry back on our account. We've got a fun filled evening lined up, haven't we, champ?' she smiled, affectionately ruffling the small boy's hair, causing him to scowl briefly at being distracted from his masterpiece.

With a final glance in the mirror to check she was presentable, and patting down one of her errant curls, she kissed her son on the top of his head and said goodbye. Stopping at a small supermarket on her way to the villa to pick up what she needed to prepare a welcome snack for her guests, she hesitated over buying the prosecco she normally bought. Remembering that Mr Lupine reportedly had a problem with booze, she opted for the alcohol free fizzy, which would be suitable for the boys too. Packing the shopping into the boot of her small car, she started to hum happily as the aroma from the freshly baked Burek temptingly filled the air.

At the villa she carefully unpacked the various meats and cheeses, alongside the savoury stuffed pie, placing them on the work surface and put the bottle of fizzy into the fridge to keep cool. Reaching up to take down her favourite serving dishes, she carefully arranged the home cured pršut, several types of salami and her favourite cheese Paški sir. Deftly chopping up the tomatoes, cucumber and peppers for the shopska salad, she dressed it with some fantastic local olive oil and topped it off with a flourish of crumbled feta.

Standing back to admire her handy work, she remembered she had also bought some Fritule, the small, sugar-coated, doughnut like pastries that Luka loved so much. She was sure Leonard's sons would love them. Tilting her head back and smiling in satisfaction at a job well done, she checked the time. She had ten minutes to tidy up the kitchen and lay out the mini feast ready for their arrival.

A short while later, she was in position by the front door, smoothing down her skirt and ready to welcome the infamous Leonard with a professional smile. Half an hour later, she was still there and there was no sign of the man. Calling the car hire company to make sure that he had picked the car up at the airport, she then called a friend who worked on the ferries that ran between Split and Supatar. "Where an earth has he got to?" she thought, having confirmed that everything was running smoothly.

On the other side of the island, Leonard was looking forlornly at an abandoned-looking building in a state of disrepair and crumbling in places. Oh my God, this can't be right, he thought, checking Google maps on his phone again. Yup, this was marked as Sea View alright. Flipping through the wad of paperwork he'd printed off with all the details for the trip, he found the number for the local concierge and tapped her number into his phone and hit the call button.

'Good evening, Isabella speaking.' The call was answered almost before it had started to ring.

'Oh, hi. Sorry, I'm having a bit of a problem. I seem to be at the wrong place… well, I hope I am!'

'Is that Mr Lupine?'

'Oh, yes, sorry, should have said, call me Leonard, please.'

'Ok Leonard, tell me exactly where you are? The route directions are fairly simple, so I'm not sure where it's gone wrong for you.'

'Ah well, hold on a mo,' Isabella heard him snapping at the persistent whine of one of the boys in the background, "Just wait a minute, Ben!"

'Ok, back with you, I didn't use the route directions. I just popped it into Google maps, thought it would be simpler.'

Running her hand through hair, Isabella realised instantly where he was, a good half hour away on the wrong side of the island. Trying to hide her irritation - this meant she would be really late getting home. She replied, 'right Leonard, I think the easiest thing is for you to head back to the port and then follow the directions that I sent you. Trying to direct you any other route may lead to more misadventures.'

'God, I'm sorry, what an idiot. I will be as quick as I can,' stammered Leonard, cutting the call and jumping back in the car.

'Right boys, a little more adventure ahead,' he joked, trying to inject some enthusiasm into his tone. Two impassive faces stared back at him. It had been a long day, and they were tired and hungry. The initial excitement had worn off quite a while ago.

'Alex, when we get back to the ferry port, I will need you to read the route directions for me. It's a very important job.' Seeing Ben's face droop even further in the rear-view mirror, he added, 'Ben, your important job is to spot any landmarks mentioned along the way to make sure we're going in the right direction this time.'

With both boys looking much happier, he programmed Supetar into his phone and headed back to the ferry port as instructed.

Just over an hour later, Isabella saw the small, green car wending its way up the road to the villa. "About bloody time," she thought, but straightened up and re-pasted the smile onto her face.

'Welcome to Brač and Sea View Cottage,' she announced to the crumpled figure unfolding from the cramped space of the driving seat. Leonard turned towards the woman waiting to greet them and gave her a wan smile.

'Thank you. Apologies again for being so late. I hope we didn't keep you from anything' he replied, opening the rear door and unbuckling the sleeping form of his youngest son.

'It's fine,' she lied. 'I'm just happy you're finally here. If you'd like to follow me, I can give you a quick tour of the villa.'

'Dad, I'm hungry,' wailed the older boy who'd climbed out of the car and was standing by his father. The poor boy looked so waif-like she felt a rush of sympathy for him and went over and crouched down in front of him.

'Hi, you must be Alex,' she grinned, putting out her hand to formally shake his. 'I'm Isabella.'

'Nice to meet you, Isabella, but I'm still hungry,' he grumbled adamantly. Laughing, she took him by the hand and led him through the house to the terrace where the welcome snack was waiting.

'Well, here's something that should solve that for you,' she teased, pointing to the beautifully laid table.

Eyes lighting up, Alex dumped his rucksack and ran towards the table, greedily digging into the nearest plates.

'Thank you so much,' he mumbled through a mouthful of bread and cheese.

'Yes, thank you,' murmured a voice right behind her, causing her to spin round and find herself standing face to face with the star himself, just a few inches away. Caught by surprise, she stood there, slightly mesmerised by his eyes. They were an unusual, almost golden colour in this light, and she could smell his masculine scent. Which was doing strange things to her stomach.

Tearing her eyes away and pulling herself together, she looked beyond him and saw Ben was asleep on the sofa where Leo had put him on his way through.

'Bless him, he must be exhausted,' she stated stupidly to cover her embarrassment, and moved a few steps back until she bumped into the chair by the table.

Still staring at her strangely, Leonard felt a little out of sorts. He was oddly rattled by this woman and he didn't know how to react. Slipping easily into his default personae he snapped, 'no need to give me a tour now, it's too late. Come back in the morning to tell me anything I need to know' and with that he turned and walked towards the kitchen, praying to God that Angelica hadn't interfered with his pre arrival shopping list and the bottle of whiskey he'd ordered would be there to greet him.

Staring after him agape, Isabella was fuming. Of all

the rude, thoughtless, arrogant people! To think she'd missed Luka's bath time for this. Becoming aware that Alex was still standing there staring at her, she turned and gave him a smile.

'Don't mind Dad,' he mumbled, wiping his mouth with a napkin. 'He's under a lot of stress and a bit tired.'

He sounded so grown up, her mood dissipated and her smile broadened. 'Never mind, I will pop back and see you in the morning and then we can talk about all the wonderful things you're going to do this week,' she proclaimed brightly to the boy, who was collecting more food onto a plate. 'Leave some for your brother,' she grinned teasingly.

'This is for Ben,' he said politely 'I'm going to cover it and put it in the fridge so he has something when he wakes up,' and he trotted off after his father.

Amazed at his thoughtfulness, she followed in his footsteps and made an effort to smile at Leonard, who was by the kitchen counter, obviously pouring a second straight shot of whiskey into his glass.

'So, I'll see you in the morning then?' She asked, trying to sound cheerful.

'Sure, whatever,' he grunted without even looking in her direction and taking a slug of the amber liquid.

☼

Restraining from slamming the door on the way out, she spent the entire drive home muttering angrily. "I shouldn't be surprised", she thought as she followed the familiar road down the mountain, "I knew he was going to be an idiot" her brain prattled on, deliberately ignoring the small bubble of thought that was trying to explore her body's immediate reaction to him.

All was quiet when she entered her house, so she carefully closed the front door and padded her way through to the terrace where Sandy was waiting for her with a glass of wine at the ready. Dropping her bag onto a chair and slumping into the sofa opposite her friend, she grabbed the glass and took a long swig before saying anything.

'How was he? I hope he behaved himself'

'Complete angel' answered Sandy 'how was he? I hope he didn't behave himself,' she tittered, throwing her head back in amusement.

'Don't even get me started on that, man. He's a complete pig! Not only did your wonderful detective get lost and keep me waiting for hours, he had the audacity to demand that I go back in the morning to give him the tour, because he couldn't be bothered to do it tonight. I've never had a guest be so rude,' she ranted, angrily taking another glug of wine, kicking off her shoes and tucking her legs under her.

'Not love at first sight, then?'

Flushing slightly at the memory of his closeness, she covered the thought with another drink. 'No, it bloody wasn't', she snapped, then stopped short. 'Sorry, Sandy, he was so foul. He really got under my skin but I shouldn't take it out on you.'

'What are friends for' assured Sandy, smiling and

topping up their glasses. 'It's a shame; I had high hopes for you two, but never mind. How were the boys?'

'Well, the little one was asleep, but the older one, Alex, was absolutely lovely. He may look like his Dad but he obviously takes after his mother. He's thoughtful, polite and remarkably charming for a 7-year-old.'

'Oh well, you can at least make sure that they have a good time even if the dad is a miserable bugger!'

By the time they had finished the bottle and Sandy was getting ready to leave, Isabella felt much calmer and ready to face the horrible man the next day. Tip toeing into Luka's bedroom, she kissed his sleeping face before taking herself thankfully to bed, trying to ignore the image of amber eyes that kept floating through her mind.

BIG SHOT

The next morning, Leonard awoke with a start. The sunlight was streaming through the window directly onto his face. Looking groggily around, he saw the empty bottle taunting him from the table and groaned. No wonder he felt so dreadful. Pulling aside the blanket he had no recollection of having, he slid off the sofa and staggered to the kitchen to turn on the coffee machine. At that moment, the boys ran in squealing.

'Morning, Dad!' shouted Ben, jumping up and down. 'Can we swim in the pool? Have you seen it, Dad? It's amazing. Can we swim? Can we? Can we, Dad?' and waving the ever present Mr Kernuffle vigorously around his head in glee.

Alex, taking in his father's ashen face, wincing at every word, took Ben by the hand. 'Come on, Benny, we need to eat something. Let's get things out for breakfast.'

Smiling gratefully at the boy, Leonard made the

effort. 'Good idea, Alex, let's eat first and then we can do some swimming.' He watched them as they shuffled out of the kitchen, battling with the Sublime Retreats robes that they insisted on wearing, even though they were swamped by them. He had to admit, despite the exorbitant 'membership fee' he'd seen on the travel companies' website, he appreciated all the extra creature comforts and luxuries they provided.

'Don't forget Isabella will be coming back this morning. I like her Dad, she's really nice,' exclaimed Alex, popping his head back in the room, causing Leonard to blanch at the memory of his rudeness to her yesterday. He wasn't sure he was up to facing her again, but guessed he'd have to.

'Yes, champ, she was nice, why don't you save a croissant for her and I'll make her some coffee when she gets here.'

'Ok, Dad,' he chirped and happily trotted off, baring plates and cutlery to set the table.

'Ben, help your brother set up. I'm going to have a quick shower.'

Standing under the blissful warm jets of water in the aqua blue bathroom, Leonard felt his body begin to recuperate, and he started to sing his latest song as he towelled himself dry.

"You make me so foolish. Why do I feel this blueness? Why am I so....."

He was looking forward to sitting down and finishing the chorus, which had been eluding him for so long. Maybe while he was here, relaxed and away from the strains of his routine, he would finally find some inspiration.

☼

Isabella had woken up early to spend some time with Luka before his grandparents arrived for the day. Usually on her guests' first day, she allowed plenty of time for her visit to answer any questions and organise the week's schedule with them. She found it made the rest of the week run smoothly if she invested time at the beginning of the holiday and, although she was not looking forward to seeing Leonard again, she was determined to be professional and make sure his holiday was perfect, no matter how rude he was.

When she arrived at Sea View Cottage she knocked, and then waited by the front door patiently. Eventually, it was answered by Alex, whose little face lit up when he saw her.

'Good morning Alex, how are you? I hope you slept well?' she asked as she followed him through the lounge, taking in the empty whiskey bottle on the table and the blanket in a crumpled heap on the floor.

'Oh yes, we all did! Dad was so tired he fell asleep on the sofa'

'I bet he did,' she said wryly.

'I found a blanket to cover him. I didn't want him to get cold,' added Alex, making her feel instantly mean for her sarcastic comment. She mentally chided herself. It wasn't the boy's fault his dad was a jerk.

Out on the terrace she saw the table was set for breakfast and the younger boy, Ben, was sitting and waiting patiently.

'Good Morning, Ben,' she beamed at him as she walked out 'I'm Isabella, but you can call me Isy if you like?'

'Good morning, Isy,' he breathed dutifully, shyly glancing away.

Looking around but seeing no sign of Leonard, she relaxed a little, and sat down at the table with the boys, easily slipping into conversation and chatting about the coming week.

When Leonard sauntered down a short while later, with just a towel wrapped around his waist, he paused in the doorway, taking in the scene. Isabella was sat, with her head thrown back in laughter, at something Ben had said, her dark curls bouncing in apparent mirth. The boys were giggling too and looked happier and more relaxed than he'd seen them in a long time. Taking a deep breath, he stepped out onto the terrace.

'Good morning, everyone,' he exclaimed, deliberately smiling at Isabella. 'Isabella, thank you for coming this morning. Can I get you some coffee?'

Yet again wrong footed by his about-face she found she was stuttering over her reply 'err, y-yes, please, that would be lovely', she could feel the blush starting to creep up her neck as she watched his bare, retreating back. She'd thought he was scrawny, but she could see he was toned and sinewy like an athlete. Trying to divert her attention, she turned back to the boys 'so, guys, what would you like to do while you're here?

Your Dad has asked me to organise some horse riding but is there something else you'd like to do?'

'Swim!' they both shouted at the same time.

Laughing with them, she smiled. 'Well, that's easy enough; you have the wonderful pool here. But you really must swim in the sea too. My son and I like to go to a beach near here and the water is amazing!' she gushed enthusiastically. 'We like to go snorkelling to see the fish.'

'I wish I could snorkel' announced Ben, 'but I'm probably too small.'

'I don't know about that. My Luka is about your age and he has learnt how to do it. Maybe get your dad to buy some masks so you can practice in the pool.'

'What are we practicing?' asked Leonard as he walked back in on the end of the conversation and placed a pretty blue cup filled with wonderful smelling coffee in front of Isabella.

'Lovely, thank you. I was just telling the boys about a great beach near here that's perfect for snorkelling'

'God, I used to love doing that as a kid. It's been years since I've had the chance! What do you say, boys, shall we give it a go?' he babbled enthusiastically, his face lighting up. Alex and Ben were delighted at the prospect. 'You should come too,' shouted Ben to Isabella. 'Bring your son, we can all snorkel together,' he cheered eagerly.

'Ah, I'm not sure we'll be able to organise that,' Leonard stuttered quickly, wanting to save Isabella the job of making excuses. 'I'm sure Isabella is far too busy with other things.'

Feeling a little hurt at his obvious disregard of the idea, even though she had been about to make excuses, she kept quiet and drank her coffee, which thankfully tasted as good as it smelt.

Alex passed her a croissant and, in an effort to move things along, she chatted amiably, mostly with the boys, for the next half an hour, discussing their plans for the week. She kept catching Leonard staring at her and felt a growing sense of tension between them, which she couldn't fathom.

Yes, he'd been foul the night before, but he was obviously making an effort towards her today, so she had softened towards him slightly. Watching him out of the corner of her eye, she saw he was scribbling on a scrap of Sublime Retreats notepaper, glancing at her in between scrawls. It was most disconcerting. Finally, pushing her chair back, she said, 'oh, by the way, I will be providing your chef service tomorrow night. What time would you like to eat?'

Looking slightly startled, Leonard stared at her wide eyed and replied, 'A woman of many talents, hey? Earlyish would be good, about 6 ok?'

'That's absolutely fine; I'll be here about 4.30 to prepare. I have a key, so you don't need to be here.'

'Doesn't your husband mind you cooking for other people?' he asked, trying to make light of the flush of pleasure he felt.

'I'm afraid Luka's dad is no longer with us. He died some time ago,' she added to soften the blow that other people felt when she told them, and determined to move the conversation on 'What about tonight?

Where were you planning to eat? Did you look at the list of restaurants in the villa book?'

'Didn't get round to reading that, I'm afraid,' murmured Leonard sheepishly. 'To be honest, I don't want to go far today. Where's the nearest place that you'd recommend, preferably somewhere with a shop nearby so we can stock up on more provisions?'

Aware that her eyes had automatically slid to the empty bottle sitting accusingly on the table inside, she tried to focus as she answered, but yet again found her eyes locked into a gaze she couldn't pull away from.

'Err, your best bet is to pop down into Bol. There are some lovely places along the harbour front there and a mini market which should have what you need.'

Feeling inexorably drawn to her large green eyes, Leonard was once again at a loss how to respond. 'Right,' he announced, abruptly standing up, knocking his chair over in the process, 'we'll see you tomorrow then' and he bent down to retrieve the chair.

Isabella was feeling confused. He blew hot and cold, charming one minute, dismissive the next. She could only assume he was naturally a brute, but just tried to cover it up sometimes, his real character coming through when he'd had enough. Well, at least she knew where she stood; she was clearly just a member of 'staff' as far as he was concerned. If that's how he wanted things, fine. She could play the subservient role for a few days if need be and to hell with him!

Stomping angrily back to her car and shutting the door with a resounding bang, she tried to put him out of her mind, but whatever she did, his amber eyes kept appearing before her, drawing her in with their hypnotic intensity. Lips pressed together, she drove down the hill to her house, where Luka was waiting for her with Ana and Ivan. At least he would be pleased to see her. She smiled at that thought.

☼

Back at the villa, Leonard and the boys were getting ready to swim in the pool. Ben had not long come out of armbands and was gung ho to show his dad how well he could swim.

'Come on, Dad, hurry up,' he shouted impatiently, hopping from foot to foot.

'Hang on there, champ. We need to put on sunscreen first, remember?'

'Aww Dad, I want to jump straight in. I can do the front crawl now. I'm really, really good, you have to watch me!'

'I will watch you all day, don't you worry,' assured Leonard, approaching with the factor 50. 'Let's just do this first; we don't want to spoil the rest of the week by getting burnt on the first day!'

Finally, they were ready to go down to the pool; the boys hightailing down the path ahead of him and leaping in with whoops of joy. 'Thank god there isn't another house for miles, he thought; it's going to be a noisy afternoon!'

Strolling down with the towels, bottles of water and his guitar and a notepad, he laid everything on one of the sunbeds and leapt in after them, causing them to shriek once again. An exhausting hour later, after playing everything from hand ball to racing, he finally excused himself and went to look at the guest house situated next to the pool.

It was a charming little studio property with a kitchenette and shower room. "This would make a fantastic studio" he thought, looking at the view from the picture windows at the front of the building. He imagined his guitars hanging on the walls and his mixing desk in the corner. He could lock himself away in here and be as creative as he liked.

It had never occurred to him, now that he was single, that he could buy somewhere with a suitable space for his writing. He would have to look into that when he got home. It would have to be somewhere with a great view, he thought. He could feel his creative juices flowing already.

But he knew that it was Isabella that had inspired him. It was being around her that had started him scribbling away feverishly as lyrics appeared in his head this morning at breakfast.

He didn't know what it was about that girl, but she had a strange effect on him every time he saw her. She made him feel so awkward and stupid and generally... 'That's it!' he shouted, triumphantly, running back outside to the sunbed. Grabbing his notepad, he wrote, "you make me foolish, why do I feel this blueness, why am I so clueless when I'm around you.' He continued to write furiously for another 10 glorious, absorbed minutes, ignoring the demands for attention from the boys in the pool.

She was his muse! He had been struggling with this chorus for so long he thought he was wasting his time, ready to give up. Yet within a few hours, she had inspired him. Thinking back to the vision of her laughing with his sons earlier, he felt a surge of emotion. Stopping mid-sentence, pen poised above the paper, he tried to examine what he was feeling. He shook his head to clear away the thoughts that were swirling through his brain.

He barely knew the woman, and it was ridiculous to think he could be feeling anything for her in this short space of time. He'd only seen her twice, for God's sake! Deciding that whatever it was, he was going to get it all on paper and finish this blasted song if it killed him. He made a few more notes before rejoining the boys in the pool. But he wasn't fully there in the moment, either in the pool or the present.

Back at home, Isabella was feeling much better. She was in her element, in the kitchen, dancing around whilst trialling out some of the dishes she was going to make tomorrow. Although Leonard had requested plain chicken, she was determined to make sure the rest of the meal was more gourmet, and Luke and his grandparents were happily willing to be her guinea pigs.

For the vegetables, she had decided to do a couple of traditional side dishes. Not knowing exactly what the boys liked, she thought a variety of dishes were more likely to ensure there'd be something they would eat.

She'd chosen Ćoravi gulaš, which was one of Luka's favourites as he loved potatoes in any form. It was a type of goulash consisting of potatoes, onions, carrots, peas, and tomato juice. She flavoured it with a little ground paprika, parsley, bay leaves, and garlic, the smells from the spices filling the room. She planned to serve it with a dollop of sour cream, just in case the spice was too much for the boys.

The second side dish was her favourite, all time, comfort food: Cvjetača sa sirom i šunkom. She loved the combination of lightly boiled cauliflower topped with slices of ham and egg, sprinkled with breadcrumbs and lashings of grated cheeses. She dotted the top with pats of butter before putting it in the oven to bake to crispy perfection, and then started on the desserts.

She found it difficult to choose just one as a favourite. The Croatians really knew what they were doing when it came to desserts, so she was glad Leonard had opted for a selection. She had decided on some Cherry Strudels, Princes krafne - the sweet creamy profiterole-like cake that Ana loved so much – and one of her personal favourites, Mađarica. The latter was usually only made for celebrations, but she couldn't resist the layered chocolate cake and made it on a regular basis.

With the last dish in the oven, Isabella checked the

time, poured a glass of red wine, and wandered across to the French doors to see what Luka was up to.

She could hear his giggling before she spotted him, running around the fruit trees being arthritically chased by Ivan while Ana stood by, watching with a smile on her face that was the embodiment of love. With the kitchen filled with the comforting aromas of home cooked food and her son playing contentedly with his grandparents in the back garden, she realised something. Despite the hole in her life left by the loss of Mateo and the shelving of her grand plans to travel the world, she was happy here. There was plenty of time for love and adventure and she chided herself for not being more grateful for everything she already had.

☼

At the villa, Leonard had finally coerced the boys out of the pool with the promise of a trip to town and a hunt for snorkeling gear. They seemed quite taken with the idea and, if he was honest, he was too. He could remember family holidays as a boy where he would spend hours in the sea, face planted firmly in the water while he marveled at the underwater life he saw there, and the thought of introducing the boys to this magical other world was extremely appealing.

Once everyone had showered and the vestiges of lunch - the remains of Isabella's welcome snack – were cleared away and dishes neatly stacked in the dish-washer, they loaded into the car, Alex slamming the door shut behind them, and headed into Bol as suggested. Driving down to the small, pretty town, they were greeted by the sparkling blue waters, restrained by a long stretch of promenade that was dotted with restaurants and souvenir shops.

As soon as he was out of the car Ben pulled his camera out and started snapping wildly and, laughing at his enthusiasm, Leonard called out, 'steady on there, fella, save some shots for the rest of the week!' Hesitating for a moment, Ben looked at his father, the internal struggle plainly writ across his little face before he decisively took one last shot and carefully put the camera back into his bag next to Mr Kernuffel.

'Although Dad needs to take some pictures too, can you remind me later, boys?'

Both boys assured him solemnly that they would, and they strolled down the length of the promenade, enjoying the rays of the afternoon sun. It was fairly quiet, obviously the lull between lunch and dinner and the boys had free rein to run, shouting out in excitement when they spotted a fish in the water, an unusually painted boat or the seductive wares on offer in the shops on the other side of the road.

Leonard managed to convince them to walk to the far end before they started back along the other side to explore the shops and choose somewhere for dinner. As they darted in and out of the shops, calling to him with every new discovery, he smiled and shook his head; they were certainly going to sleep tonight.

The shops were tightly packed emporiums of delight for a small boy. Gaudily coloured fridge magnets abound, handmade wooden toys and instruments inviting exploration and noise, and rows of plastic geegaws that Leonard made a mental note not to let them buy. One shop was selling locally made soaps and the overriding smell of lavender in the small emporium sharply brought back memories of his grandmother, who he hadn't thought about in years. He had spent all his summer holidays with her at her riding stables in Ireland; he had fond memories of those times which, although were tainted by the thought of his parents' apparent need to be free of him, were his happiest memories of childhood.

'Dad, Dad' called out Alex, 'we should totally buy some soaps for mum, she would love them'

Thinking that the last thing Rennie would like was some soap without the stamp La Chatelaine on it he responded noncommittally 'let's just look for now, we can come back later in the week and do a present shop for everyone once we have a good idea what's available.' That seemed to satisfy them and they were soon distracted by the next shop, which had beach accessories, and it wasn't long until all three of them were armed with snorkeling equipment as well as 'floaties' for the pool.

Alex picked a huge, industrial looking doughnut shaped inflatable whilst Ben went for one in the shape of a tiger, his current favourite animal. Leonard was more reserved with a traditional lilo, although it did have a cup holder moulded into it and was a startling pink colour. Not relishing the idea of trying to blow them up - he wasn't sure his lungs were up to it - Leonard was elated when the shopkeeper told him he could stop at the petrol station on the way out of town and get them filled with air there.

They were flagging a bit by this stage, so they decided it was time for dinner and picked a restaurant set in the arches of the medieval-looking wall that ran along the tail end of the promenade. After ordering cokes for the boys and opting to try the local beer, Ozujsko, which was on draft, they poured over the menus.

Happy to see they had a kids' menu with some more familiar items, the boys soon chose their favourites - chicken nuggets and a hamburger, while Leonard opted for the fish of the day which turned out to be the most amazing tuna he had ever eaten. They sat for a while after they had finished. Alex and Ben slowly scooping their way through the complimentary ice cream that had been brought to the table and Leonard treating himself to another ice cold beer.

Feeling remarkably content, Leonard stretched out his long legs and savoured the sensation. Moments like this seemed non-existent in his life, he really was going to have to do something about that. He wasn't sure what or how, but he knew he had to shake things up and get out of the miserable rut his life was currently in.

Finally deciding it was time to start making their way home as the sun began to sink towards the horizon, causing the limestone walls to glow; Leonard paid the bill and left a hefty tip in gratitude to the wonderful time and food they had had. They walked, more slowly now and with less squealing, back towards Karl, who was thankfully parked where they had left him, stopping for provisions on the way.

At the small supermarket they stocked up on local cheeses, hams and bread and croissants for tomorrow's breakfast and Leonard, ignoring the whisky that was calling his name, picked up a couple of bottles of local red wine to try which felt a little less desperate somehow. At the counter, he gave in to the boy's request for chocolate, and threw a couple of bars of what looked by the images to be fruit and nut into his basket to satisfy their need for something sweet.

Remembering at the last minute about blowing up the pool toys, Leonard veered off into the petrol station and managed to make himself understood by dint of waving the toys in front of the attendant and miming blowing in such a way he had the boys in stitches.

'The air is over there' announced the attendant in perfect English, causing him a flush of embarrassment and a reminder that he hadn't even learnt how to say thank you in Croatian yet.

Once he'd finally got them inflated, he manhandled them back to the car, battling the early evening breeze. And stopped a little short of the car as it dawned on him, for all Karl's attributes, size wasn't one of them.

'Where are we going to put them?' asked Alex, looking doubtfully at the large ring that had been his choice of floatie and then back at the space left in the car next to them.

'Umm, I'm not entirely sure, son,' muttered Leonard, choosing to ignore the snorts coming from the attendant, who was obviously enjoying the show. Trying to wedge in the doughnut first, as this was the largest, with much huffing and puffing, Leonard soon realised he was onto a nonstarter. He could get it in the backseat, but not with his children as well.

Pausing to reflect on the challenge in front of him and catch his breath, Leonard felt a tug on his t-shirt, and, looking down onto the solemn face of his youngest, he smiled 'don't worry, Benny, Daddy will work it out'

'I know you will, Dad, I was just going to say why don't we let a little bit of puff out, you know, just enough so they can squidge in?'

Marvelling at the remarkable sense of his child he laughed and crowed 'you know what, Benny, you are absolutely spot on, and that's a brilliant idea!' and, following the suggestion, they finally managed to force the toys into the car, albeit with the boys faces pressed up against the windows, steaming them up, and resumed the journey back up to the villa.

Finally, they pulled into the drive and up to the villa and were expelled out of the car with relief. Deciding to leave the inflatables in situ until tomorrow, Leonard pulled the bags of shopping from the boot and walked up to the front door, happily chatting with the boys about their plans for tomorrow.

And then he realised, looking at that firmly closed door, that he had no idea where the key was. With a familiar, sinking feeling he turned to Alex 'when we left, Alex, when you shut the door, what did you do with the key?'

Alex looked up at him, panic flashing across his face. 'What key? I didn't know I was in charge of the key,' he quavered, voice escalating in fear and tears starting to well up in his eyes. Feeling guilty, he immediately knelt down and gave the boy a hug.

'Don't worry, Alex, you were not in charge. Daddy is, well, he's supposed to be, but it appears I have been a bit silly and didn't think about it when we left.'

☀

Isabella and Ana sat on the terrace talking amiably, finishing off the wine they had had with dinner while Ivan took his turn at the nightly bedtime story ritual. Luka loved it when his grandpa read to him; he was much more committed to making all the noises and strange voices that his favourite book required.

As Isabella sat, staring off into the distance, lost in her own thoughts, she didn't notice Ana looking at her until the woman suddenly asked, 'tell me dragi, are you happy here?'

Startled that the older woman had picked up on the thoughts that had been running around her head these last days, she paused before answering, wanting to be honest without upsetting this woman who'd been her rock of support for so long.

'I can honestly say that I am,' responded Isabella, looking seriously at Ana and pushing her ever errant curls away from her eyes. 'I will admit that I sometimes feel the desire to go travelling again, but not at the expense of my son. He is my world and whatever makes him happy makes me happy.'

Ana nodded knowingly. This she could understand, but she also knew as a woman there was more to life. 'And what about love? It's been a long time since Mateo left us...' The look of pain that flitted across Ana's face brought tears to Isabella's eyes. She couldn't imagine what that felt like, losing her son was unfathomable. She shifted uncomfortably in her seat, not sure about the direction this conversation was taking.

When she didn't respond, Ana continued, 'I know you loved Mateo and I know you will never forget him, but don't think that if you open yourself up to meet someone else that you will be betraying his memory. Betraying his memory would be not living your life, not being as happy as you can be every single day, whatever that entails,' she finished firmly, but with a smile on her weathered face.

The words sank in, but Isabella didn't know how to respond. The guilt she felt whenever her loneliness led her to daydream about having someone to share her life with was deeply ingrained, partly due to the loyalty she felt towards these people.

Her phone suddenly shrilled, and she thankfully swooped it off the table, wondering who would be calling at this time of night. One glance at the screen let her know it was her annoying villa guest and all thoughts of the conversation disappeared as she answered curtly.

'Isabella speaking, how can I help you, Mr Lupine?'

'Oh, hello, call me Leonard, please,' he stuttered

'OK, Leonard, what can I do for you this evening?' she responded, keeping her icy demeanour despite how nervous and shy he sounded.

'I'm afraid we're in somewhat of a pickle,' he mumbled, causing a smile to leap involuntarily to her lips. 'We went out this evening - had a lovely time in Bol, by the way, thank you for that recommendation. But we've just gotten back, and it appears we have left the key in the villa...' he trailed off.

Sighing deeply as she knew that this meant she would have to go out again and take the spare key up to them, she tried to keep her voice professional and offered 'not to worry, Leonard, I have a spare I can bring you. It will take me...' she glanced at the time 'about half an hour to get to you, hang tight and I will be there as quick as I can.'

She looked at Ana and groused, 'I'm sorry, as you probably gathered I have to go to the villa. Are you OK to stay until I get back?'

'Of course, of course. I don't think Luka is done with his grandpa yet anyway, so it's not a problem' she laughed as Isabella pulled on her cardigan and grabbed her bag from the hooks by the front door. 'And think about what I said, you are too young to live like a widow!'

On the drive up the mountain, Isabella did think about what Ana had expressed, her surprise at the turn of the conversation swiftly taken over by a mixed bag of emotions. Fear, sadness and guilt all whirled around and around, but she felt and focused on a new feeling, a little, tiny spark of hope that sent a flutter of excitement through her. The idea of having someone to share her life with was thrilling. She had no idea where this was leading, but it was the first time she had felt like this in a long time, and she was determined not to let it go.

When she arrived at the villa, Leonard was sitting forlornly on the wall by the front door, gazing up at the stars with Alex, pointing out the constellations. Standing up to greet her with an embarrassed smile on his face, he commented, 'thank you so, so much for coming to our rescue. I can't believe what an idiot I've been!'

Thinking that this guy was constantly being an idiot she replied 'Not to worry, it's what I'm here for' and, pulling the keys out of her bag, walked to the door and opened it 'Voila' she announced, looking around 'where's Ben by the way?'

Glancing around and seeing no sign of his smallest son, he called out, 'Ben, Ben, where are you?'

'In here, Dad,' piped a small voice from the villa. Looking confused, Leonard ran in, closely followed by Alex and Isabella, to be greeted by the sight of Ben, smiling gaily and covered in chocolate.

'How on earth did you get in here' demanded Leonard, to which Ben, mouth still full of chocolate, just pointed, with a besmeared Mr Kernuffle dangling from his hand, at the patio doors which were wide open.

Isabella didn't know whether to laugh or cry, but the look of absolute horror on Leonard's face decided it for her and she threw her head back in peals of laughter. Leonard looked on dumbstruck, for about thirty seconds, before her infectious laughter broke through his complete mortification and he bent over, slapping his thighs as he joined in with her mirth.

Wiping the tears from his eyes, he remarked, 'I am so, so sorry. I cannot believe I didn't think to check the other doors and stuff. I just panicked. Oh, my god what an idiot' he smiled at her.

'The great detective, huh?' she grinned at him. 'I guess you won't be putting this on Instagram!' and she burst out laughing again. Walking into the kitchen and grabbing some paper towels to wipe Ben's face, he looked over his shoulder at her.

'Look, can I offer you a glass of wine or something? To make up for your wasted journey?'

Seeing him look so normal, relaxed and laughing with his sons, made Isabella realise that the idea or spending a little longer in his company no longer filled her with dread. 'I wouldn't mind a coffee?' she ventured, smiling tentatively, aware that she had already had enough wine for one day.

Leonard nodded his assent, not even noticing that the desperate desire he had had for alcohol only moments ago had disappeared, and moved back into the kitchen to turn on the coffee machine.

A short while later they were sitting at the table outside, the boys falling over themselves to gleefully regale her with the story of the inflatables and proudly showing them off after insisting on dragging them out of the car. When Isabella glanced at the time, she was amazed to see how late it was and stood up to take her leave, aware that she should get back to Luka.

Watching her put her cardigan back on, Leonard realised he didn't want this moment to end, didn't want this woman to leave, and abruptly blurted out, 'what should we do tomorrow?' causing her to stop mid-buttoning and look at him.

'Well, what did you have in mind? I know Ben and Alex will spend all day in the pool if you let them, but it would be a shame not to see more of the island while you are here'

'Exactly! Just what I was thinking' he proclaimed, a little loudly even to his ears and, ignoring the boy's protestations about leaving the pool even for a minute, he continued, 'where do you suggest?'

'I think you should travel down to Sumartin. It's not too far, let me show you on the map,' she replied, then, to Alex who was still grumbling about inflatables and pool time 'Alex, could you pop and get me the map from the villa book? I think I better show you where it is you are going so Dad doesn't get lost!'

Immediately heartened by being put in charge, Alex dutifully went inside to get the map. Chuckling in admiration at her skilful management of his children's temperaments, he mouthed 'thank you' across the table and gave her a smile that made her legs go weak.

Determined to ignore her body's ridiculous reaction to a simple smile, she spread the map out onto the table, bending down and smoothing it out to and show Alex where they were going. As she told the boys about the lovely harbour front and the boat trip they could take from there, she became painfully aware of Leonard's presence next to her. Heat seemed to be radiating off him and being absorbed wantonly by her body like some kind of demented Reiki. Confused, she straightened up suddenly.

'Look, I really have to go,' she pronounced with an embarrassed smile, 'I have to get back to my son.'

'Of course, I'm sorry, we have kept you far too long,' noted Leonard stiltedly, feeling only sorry that she was leaving but not being able to think of one good reason to keep her any longer.

'Come on, boys, let's let Isabella get home and it's time for you two to go to bed' he started, which was followed by the inevitable chorus of 'aww Dad' which made Isabella smile.

'Off you go, boys, and don't forget, I will see you tomorrow. I'm coming to cook for you so you can tell me all about your day when I get here.'

Brightening up at the thought that he would be seeing her again tomorrow, Leonard walked with her to the front door. 'Thank you again for rescuing us,' he chuckled shamefacedly 'and again, I'm sorry for dragging you out.'

Peering up at him through her curls, Isabella smiled. 'Not a problem, have a great day tomorrow and I will see you at about 4:30 for the cooking extravaganza!'

'I'm looking forward to it,' revealed Leonard quietly, gazing intently into her eyes, unable to drag his eyes away. Silence fell between them and a hundred years passed, neither of them able to move. Isabella suddenly snapped to attention, dispelling the tension that had come up between them.

'OK, night' she called, hurrying back to her car so she could speed away from this weird situation and the strange emotions she was feeling.

"Huh…" thought Leonard as the wheels spun and she sped down the drive. She obviously can't get away quick enough! Stupid, stupid! As if a wonderful, sweet woman like that would have any interest in a grumpy old git like me. Clenching his fists at his stupidity, he walked back into the villa to put his boys to bed and finally open that bottle of wine.

THE CAPTAIN

Despite the late night, Leonard and the boys were up early. Excited by the idea of going out on a boat, Alex and Ben woke him up with breakfast in bed. Thankful that he had done no more than sip at his glass of wine last night, pondering the state of his life before giving it up as a bad job and going up to bed, Leonard was feeling refreshed and determined to enjoy the day with his sons. Smiling at their anticipation for the day ahead, he munched through the croissant with its sloppily applied jam as quickly as he could while they collected their things, ready to start their day.

The short, half-hour drive to Sumartin, which Alex competently directed them to, took them through the centre of the island and Leonard marvelled at how clean and beautiful everywhere was. All the buildings that they saw seemed pristine, and there was no sign of litter anywhere. He loved living in London but he realised how grim the city appeared, especially in the winter, and the rolling landscape of this charming, small island emphasised how hemmed in the confines of the city made him feel.

He had never imagined living anywhere else up until now, but this holiday was showing him that there were definitely changes he needed to make in his life and that he needed to start being more proactive rather than just riding the waves that crashed upon him regularly. Tucking that thought away for further exploration, he concentrated on the here and now as they approached their destination.

As the road wound its way down into the pretty harbourfront they were greeted by a horseshoe-shaped bay, the sea twinkling invitingly, a shocking blue after all the shades of green that the coun-tryside they had driven through provided, and low-level buildings blending seamlessly in, dominated by the impressive church spire standing proudly in the centre of the village. It seemed like a quiet, relaxed-looking place. No hustle and bustle here, just small clusters of locals gathered at the various simple cafés on the waterfront, sipping coffees and no doubt dis-cussing the vital gossip of the day, but little else in the way of activity.

They parked up by the seafront and strolled down towards where the hire boats were tied up, bobbing away in tidy rows, waiting for their next customers. Taking Isabella's advice, they stopped off on the way at the small mini-market with a bakery and stocked up on water and sandwiches to see them through their trip. Suitably prepared, they found the owner of the boats by means of standing in front of them looking lost, which soon brought him running from the café where he'd been seated, and a short negotiation later and they were climbing into a small, white, 30hp boat with a smart, dark blue sun canopy.

Although Leonard was a little nervous - he hadn't been on a boat since he was a boy - the instructions he received seemed simple enough and, after manoeuvring carefully out of the harbour, he felt his confidence grow as they motored along the coast, following the map provided, to get to a beach inaccessible by car where they could swim.

Even though the sea was amazingly calm, as promised, the boat bounced gently across the swell with rhythmic bumps and, with the wind whipping his hair as he increased the revs, Leonard let out a whoop; he hadn't felt this alive in a long time. Grinning at the boys perched at the front, safely ensconced in their life jackets and beaming widely despite their small hands ferociously gripping onto the sides, he felt truly happy.

He let both of his sons have a turn at the wheel, enjoying their thrill at such a responsibility but staying close by just in case, although they both took to it like ducks to water and seemed to have an instinct for riding the swell. When it looked like they were nearing their destination, he took over and started angling the boat nearer to the coast, not wanting to miss the small bay they were aiming for. After a few minutes, he spotted it and, pointing it out to the boys, carefully steered towards it.

Reducing his speed as he motored slowly into the small, deserted bay hemmed by a tiny golden beach, he threw the anchor overboard with some effort and, as the boat came to a gentle stop, he jumped into the water which came up to his swimming shorts and secured the painter to a craggy rock.

'Come on, boys,' he called, 'grab your snorkels and let's do this!'

They didn't need much encouragement. Alex leapt straight in and, after a moment's hesitation, Ben followed suit, doggy paddling over to his dad for help to put on his snorkel. They spent the following hour mastering the art of snorkelling. Strangely, Ben took to it straight away, and it was Alex who struggled, his fear of inhaling water getting the better of him. But eventually his desire not to be bested by his little brother won out and they were soon swimming along together, marvelling at the shoals of tiny, colourful fish, the spikey black sea urchins and the discovery of a family of crabs living on the rocks that edged the bay.

When they took a break for something to eat, Leonard retrieved the cool box provided with the boat where they had stored their provisions, and they sat happily on the sand, munching away on the sandwiches and crisps and talking excitedly about what they had seen.

Finishing off his bottle of water and reaching for another, Alex looked at Leonard and challenged, 'Dad, why can't we stay with you all the time? It's much more fun with you.' To which Ben nodded in serious agreement, crumbs falling from his mouth.

Blindsided, Leonard took another bite of his sandwich, thoughtfully chewing to gain time. He always tried to be careful about what he said with regards to his ex-wife. He knew it didn't help the situation to be disparaging or encourage them to take sides.

'I am super happy to hear you are enjoying yourself, Alex' he assured the boys, who were both now looking at him intently, 'But you have to remember that this is a holiday, I don't usually do fun things like this. In fact, my life is incredibly boring most of the time; I don't think you'd enjoy it. And besides, your mum would miss you too much.' He added over their protestations.

'Huh,' they both grumbled in unison, which would have been comical if it weren't for the matter at hand.

'What does that mean' he asked, not sure what to make of their reaction. Both boys now seemed incapable of meeting his eyes and were determinedly looking everywhere but at him. Ben choosing to be deeply involved in scraping the last morsels out of his crisp packet and Alex opting for gazing out at the sea with amazing intensity.

'Come on, boys, if you have something to say just spit it out. You know there is nothing you can't say to me,' he said evenly, smiling to encourage them to speak. Afraid of what they would say, but knowing he had to continue down this rabbit hole.

'It's just...' Alex began, then stopped, obviously searching for the words.

'Mum doesn't have time for us, now she has John,' blurted out Ben chirpily, trying to wipe away the

crumbs that had stuck to his damp chest and completely oblivious to his brother's attempts at tact.

'I'm sure that's not true,' hesitated Leonard carefully, 'your mum is very busy, just like me. I'm sure she
spends as much time as she can with you. But we both
have work and stuff, things we can't avoid.'

Alex looked at his dad seriously 'do you know how
many times we have seen her in the last two weeks?'
he asked, sounding far too grown up. 'Twice', he
added, 'Just twice when she came to say goodnight to
us before going out to a party or whatever. The rest of
the time we are with the nanny or sent down to Nanny
and Grandpas' when the nanny has a day off.'

Leonard took this news in and kept the smile on his
face as he probed further 'and how long has it been
like this? Maybe Mum has just been really busy? She
has a lot going on right now with the new record and
her engagement and everything,' he asked, knowing
small boy's ability to exaggerate.

'Pretty much all the time now,' divulged Alex. 'The
last time we spent any proper time together was on
my birthday last month.'

Feeling incredibly guilty - he could remember not
being able to make it for Alex's birthday because he
was filming - he proffered carefully 'Well that's nice,
she took time out to be with you on your special day',
fervently hoping the boy would not comment on his
absence.

'It was only because our nanny walked out the day
before. Mum was furious. Then we had to go to Nanny
and Grandpa for a whole week while she tried to find

another one. No one likes to stay very long, I'm not sure why. It's a real shame. We liked Annabel.'

Leonard, who had only a hazy recollection of the woman concerned, could easily imagine why this was. Rennie was impossible to live with; working for her must be a nightmare. He shuddered at the thought and took a moment to marshal his thoughts.

'Well, I'll tell you what, I would love to spend more time with you too, and although I can't promise anything about timings, I do promise to talk to mum when we get back home and see what we can do, ok?'

Both boys nodded happily and in an effort to change the conversation he chortled, 'right, I think it's time for me to take some pictures for Instagram. You two monkeys were supposed to remind me, weren't you?!' and he pulled his phone out of his bag as they giggled in acknowledgement of their lapse. 'OK, you can both take turns taking photos. Where do you think I should stand?'

'In the sea!' shouted Ben gleefully, and they spent the next half an hour blissfully getting their dad to make stupid poses and filling up the memory of his phone with endless photos. Swiping through them when they'd finished, Leonard realised there was probably only one or two that he could send for Sublime Retreats to use, but it was a start. He'd have to take some more later, at the villa, maybe of the dinner.

The thought of dinner inexorably brought the image of Isabella to his mind, pushing her hair out of her eyes and laughing at him. The idea of seeing her again compelled him and he asked, 'how about we pack up and go home? Those inflatables are waiting for their maiden voyage,' he added before they could protest.

☼

Isabella had spent a sleepless night, tossing and turning as her brain relived the previous evening with Leonard over and over and over again. Especially those final, thrilling moments, that strange intensity that had developed between them. If she didn't know better, she would think he had been about to kiss her.

This thought sent nervous butterflies cavorting through her entire body before her brain stamped down on them cruelly for being so wilful, and then the thought process started all over again. So she was still a little bleary looking, despite lashings of Touche Éclat, when she met Sandy for coffee in Bol the next morning.

'What's up with you?' inquired Sandy without preamble as she arrived at the terrace table, dumping her bag on a chair and pulling out the one next to it to sit on, 'you look like something the cat dragged in, and that's putting it mildly!'

'Oh, that idiot at the villa locked himself out last night and I had to go up,' she replied glibly, trying to look nonchalant and put Sandy off the scent, but to no avail.

'Really?' she taunted, stretching the word out and making it sound lascivious, as only Sandy could. 'And how is the luscious Leonard?'

'Well, stupid obviously' complained Isabella primly, but not before a telling smile flew across her face, brightening it up in a way that no miracle makeup ever could.

'Tell me more,' probed Sandy, looking intently at her friend, sensing that something exciting was about to be revealed. Just then, the waiter came to the table to take their orders, both of them opting for cold coffees, as it was such a warm day. Not to be put off by a minor distraction. 'So what happened?' she insisted.

Although she had sworn that she wasn't going to mention anything, especially to Sandy, who would no doubt make a mountain out of a molehill, Isabella found herself unable to restrain the flow of words any longer.

'Well, it turned out that the back door was open the whole time, so of course he felt bad for dragging me out. So then he offered me a drink, I opted for coffee, obviously. And then we sat and chatted. His boys are so sweet' she rambled on in the face of Sandy's knowing stare 'and then...' she paused 'and then when I was leaving there was this strange moment' she finished lamely.

'Strange?!' Sandy squeaked 'what do you mean strange?' she quizzed, leaning forward avidly and nearly knocking over the coffees that she had not noticed were about to be served. 'Thank you,' she snapped at the waiter, waving him away rather rudely. 'Tell me exactly what happened' she demanded, clutching her glass for dear life.

'Hard to describe really,' replied Isabella frustratingly.

'Well, try!'

'Well, there was this long moment, it felt like forever, where he was gazing into my eyes. His eyes are a remarkable amber shade, you know; they look different depending on the light. Anyway, it was like one of those scenes from a film, when you just know they are going to kiss.'

'Oh my God!' shouted Sandy. 'So, what happened next?'

'I said goodnight, got into my car and drove home,' explained Isabella, with her forehead bunched up in puzzlement at the question. Sandy slapped the table with the palm of one hand and sat back with a thud that made her chair rock.

'You are telling me that one of the hottest TV stars of our time was about to kiss you and you just left?' She asked unbelievingly, her eyes blinking rapidly in amazement at the weirdness of her friend.

'I didn't say he was going to kiss me,' stated Isabella adamantly 'I just said it felt like one of those moments. Besides, he's a client here on holiday. What would be the point?'

'Firstly, if it felt like it, then it was IT,' advised Sandy knowingly 'and secondly, all that "he's a client, here on holiday" blah, blah, blah means you've actually thought about it. You've actually considered snogging Leonard Lupine!' she crowed triumphantly, looking at her friend, daring her to dispute this fact.

Knowing when she was beaten Isabella smiled widely, 'I must confess that it did play on my mind for a while last night' she admitted, underplaying the hours of restlessness she had been tormented by. 'But on reflection, I think it was just a reaction after speaking with Ana. We had the strangest conversation last night; I think she was basically telling me to find myself another fella'

'Good for her!' piped Sandy, interrupting her.

Carrying on as if Sandy hadn't uttered a word, 'The phone rang whilst we were talking, so I'm sure my mind was thinking about that when all this happened. And although I am prepared to admit that maybe I am ready for some love in my life, I am equally prepared to say that it most definitely won't be with Leonard. He's an arse most of the time; he lives in London and has a messy divorce behind him. It's all baggage I don't need.'

'I didn't say you have to marry him, you silly woman, but a holiday fling might be just what you both need,' interjected Sandy in-between sips of her coffee. 'A little wake up call for you and your body and a little stress release for him,' she teased, winking whilst grasping the straw to her drink firmly in her mouth.

'You are incorrigible,' chuckled Isabella, laughing, 'but no, I've decided to put it out of my mind as far as he's concerned and be nothing but professional tonight when I am cooking. I'll make it clear to him that it's not on the cards,' she added firmly, ignoring the little voice inside her that was pointing out how difficult this was going to be.

☼

When she arrived at the villa that afternoon and started to unpack all the cooking supplies from the boot of her car, she smiled as she heard the whoops and splashes coming from the pool. The boys were obviously having a whale of a time down there. Letting herself in, she carried everything into the kitchen, surprised to see how clean and tidy everything was.

Usually people on holiday became extremely lax; knowing that the maid will clean up after them, so it was a relief to see the kitchen was ready for her to start cooking straight away. She'd heard horror stories from her chefs about dishwashers full of dirty crockery and cutlery on arrival, let alone debris cast across the work surfaces, meaning a huge delay in their start time and complaints from guests about late service.

Taking a moment to savour the view she loved so much before steeling herself to see him, she walked purposefully down to the pool to make her presence known before she started.

'Good afternoon,' she called loudly over the hubbub the two boys were making. 'Just wanted to let you know I'm here,' she added pointlessly.

'Hi, Isy,' both boys called as they prepared to jump back into the pool. Leonard, who had been blissfully bobbing on his Lilo, mentally working on his song, sat up, startled by the sound of her voice and, falling slowly over sideways, grappled ungainly with the slippery plastic in an effort to stay upright and failed miserably. Coming up for air, choking out the chlorinated water, eyes streaming, he tried to appear nonchalant as he shook the water from his face.

'Hi Isabella, how are you today?'

Doing her best to hide her laughter, she replied good-naturedly. 'I'm good, thank you; I hope you guys enjoyed Sumartin?'

'It was amazing,' shouted Ben, who was pulling his small form out of the pool with some effort, his little legs scrabbling ineffectually on the mosaic tiles.

Instinctively going over to help him, she reached her hand down to pull him out, the other grabbing one of the towels on the lounger next to her. Wrapping it around him and automatically beginning to dry him, she asked, 'what did you like best, Ben?'

Looking serious for a moment, then smiling, he announced, 'I liked it all. The boat was amazing, I drove it and I learnt how to snorkel and Dad was very silly and we took lots of photos. He's gonna put them on Insta thingy,' he added proudly.

Smiling at a grimacing Leonard over the top of the boy's head, she stated wickedly, 'are you now? I would very much like to see those photos, Ben.'

Alex, who had walked over with his towel, obviously not wanting to be left out, proclaimed, 'I took the best ones. When he fell off the boat, I got him just hitting the water!' he beamed proudly.

Laughing out loud this time, she looked back at Leonard's horrified face. 'Imagine that,' she giggled as their eyes locked. Standing up and reminding herself of her earlier statement she commented 'I'm going to go and prepare some lovely food for you all, it will be ready at about 6 if that's still ok?' and turned and started to walk purposefully back towards the villa, the word 'focus' reverberating through her head with every step she took.

Feeling slightly bereft that she had left so quickly and cursing for being so uncool when she arrived, Leonard calculated how much more time he could allow the kids to play in the pool before going in, to be near to her, without too much protesting on their part.

'OK boys, another fifteen minutes, then we all need to go and have showers. I want you both to help set the table as a surprise for Isabella.'

'That's OK, Dad, we can go in now,' answered Alex hurriedly. 'The sooner we get dressed, the sooner we can help her.'

Surprised by his sons' reaction and noticing that Ben was obviously of the same mind as he started to pick up his goggles and Mr Kernuffle and prepared to walk back up to the house, he taunted, 'Excellent, well done, you two. Last one there is a sissy!' and hared up the path followed by two giggling boys.

As they exploded noisily into the villa, Isabella stuck her head out of the kitchen.

'Everything alright?' she enquired, grinning at them. Taking in her bright pink apron, hair wrapped around what looked like a pen in a messy bun leaning precariously to one side, Leonard felt an alarming pang of desire shoot through him. She looked utterly gorgeous.

'Everything is just perfect,' he answered, gazing at

her in a way that let her know exactly what was going through his mind.

Startled and blushing furiously, she dived back into the kitchen to hide, calling 'I'll leave you to it then'. Leaning on the worktop to support her wobbly legs, Isabella gave herself a stern talking to. 'You will be strong' she scolded, 'you will not let this ridiculous man get the better of your common sense.' Duly berated, she started to cut up the cauliflower for her favourite side dish.

An hour later, everything prepared and baking or simmering as it should, she ventured out to set the table for the meal, aware that it had been quiet out there for a while. Walking out onto the terrace she was greeted by the sight of a perfectly laid table, with candles flickering prettily along its length and Ben in the process of stuffing some wildflowers he'd obviously plucked from the garden into a small vase, barely up to the task.

'Oh, my goodness, this all looks incredible,' she exclaimed to the two boys who were now standing to one side, beaming proudly. 'Was this your idea?' she asked Alex, thinking how thoughtful the boy was to save her a time-consuming job.

'Actually, Dad suggested it,' he conceded begrudgingly, 'but we did all the work,' making it clear where all praise should be going.

'Well thank you, you've done an excellent job.' She smiled at them. 'Where is your dad, by the way? It won't be long until food is ready.'

'He took his guitar somewhere,' answered Ben,

looking around and cocking one ear to follow the faint sound of music that only now registered to her ears. Following the direction of the music around the side of the villa to the small sheltered alcove there, she stopped in her tracks as she heard the most wonderful music being played and then a soulful voice singing.

"*You make me so foolish. Why do I feel this blueness? Why am I so clueless when I'm around you?*"

"*Every time I see you, I want to stay near you. I never want to leave you or these moments that we share.*"

'I didn't know that you could sing,' observed Isabella into the pause that followed and startling Leonard for the second time that day, causing him to drop his guitar with a loud, if discordant, clang.

'Oh, hi.' he apologised 'I didn't see you there, I hope I wasn't disturbing you?'

'Not at all, I just came to let you know that food will be ready soon,' stated Isabella, looking at him strangely. 'That was a lovely song. Who's it by?'

'Erm, actually, I wrote it,' admitted Leonard sheepishly 'well, I'm trying to,' he continued. 'It's been a bit of a challenge, but it seems to be falling into place now,' he added with a small smile of wonder.

Isabella was taken aback by this news. She hadn't thought about the man beyond the tabloid headlines she had read before his arrival and what little she had seen of him since he'd been here. It hadn't occurred to her that there might be more to him than an actor with a bad reputation and an accident-prone character, and if he really had written those lyrics, then he obviously had a sensitive side that was carefully, completely, hidden from the world. She wondered why but, reminding herself that it was none of her business, she confirmed 'well, it was lovely. I hope you manage to finish it. I'll send one of the boys to get you when I'm serving up,' and smartly turned around and walked away.

Leonard sat staring into the distance, watching the final rays of the setting sun, and pondered why he felt so happy that Isabella had called his song lovely. Remembering the words 'silly little songs' that he'd heard from Angelica just days before, would he have felt so warm and content if she had remarked that his song was lovely? He didn't think so and, shaking his head in amusement at the thought of his agent saying anything so encouraging, he decided he wasn't going to get anything else written tonight when all he wanted was to join the others, so he stood, picked up his guitar and wandered back around to be with them.

The evening that followed was a combination of agony and ecstasy for both of them. Isabella desperately trying to maintain a professional distance but delighting in the glances she caught from him, the thrill of the accidental brushing of hands when passing a serving plate. Leonard doing his best not to stare at her, keep the conversation flowing naturally with his boys and hide his disappointment when Isabella refused to join them to eat, insisting she was their cook and going back into the kitchen to clean up the debris from the preparations.

The meal was exquisite. Even Alex and Ben, who usually turned their noses up at anything they didn't recognise, wolfed down large portions of everything and wiped their plates clean. Despite his desire to go into the kitchen, Leonard let the boys carry out their unusual urge to be helpful and take the dishes in to Isabella. But when he heard the sounds of chatter and laughter coming from inside, he couldn't resist any longer and went in to join them. The boys and Isabella had formed a line and were rinsing then stacking the plates in the dishwasher, laughing together easily.

'Any help needed in here? He asked hopefully.

'We're pretty much done,' replied Isabella, 'but you can take that plate with the desserts out. We'll be there in a minute.'

Feeling dismissed, he did as he was told and went back out and sat, feeling lonely, at the table, pouring another large glass of wine and taking a big slug. "To hell with her," he thought angrily as more sounds of merriment came from inside, "who needs this non-sense" and drained the rest of the glass before pouring himself another.

In the kitchen, Isabella was discussing the next day with the boys. 'Your Dad has planned a day at the villa tomorrow so you can spend all day in the pool,' she responded to the animated duo.

'Are you going to come and watch us diving in?' asked Ben sweetly.

She laughed and ruffled his short, blonde hair, so similar to his father's. 'Not tomorrow,' she said. 'I have a day off from work, so I will be going to the beach with my son Luka to watch him diving in, no doubt. You remember I told you about our favourite beach?'

'Oh, yes,' remarked Alex artfully, 'what was it called again?'

'Zlatni Rat,' she replied. 'There's a great beach bar there where we like to hang out. Luke loves the chips that they make,' she exclaimed.

Muttering the name to himself under his breath, Alex smiled as they made their way out to the table. It was obvious by his glassy-eyed stare that Leonard had been quietly enjoying his wine whilst they were busy in the kitchen. Looking up, but struggling to focus on her, he slurred, 'you may as well go now; the boys can clear up once they've finished with dessert. We wouldn't want to keep you longer than necessary.'

Feeling hurt and angered, especially as she had been planning to take him up on his earlier offer of a glass, but also seeing the crestfallen looks of the two small boys, she bit back an angry retort and countered 'it's not a problem, I'm quite happy to finish tidying up. It's all part of the service,' she added curtly.

'Just go,' growled Leonard, sounding like his alter ego. 'There's no need for you to stay.'

Fuming, Isabella collected her things from the kitchen, angrily slamming shut kitchen cupboards as she put away the last of the things she had used when cooking. "Of all the mean-spirited, pretentious..." Her brain stopped at that point, not even wanting to swear in the privacy of her mind.

Popping her head out the door 'Right, I won't see

you tomorrow as it's my day off, but I will meet you the next day to take you to the horse riding centre.'

Alex carefully put down his spoon and stood up to walk with her to the door.

'Thank you for dinner. It was yummy,' he said. 'And sorry about Dad, he gets like that sometimes,' he added apologetically.

Feeling bad for the boy, Isabella smiled gently. 'I'm glad you enjoyed the food. Will you be alright?'

Apparently understanding, Alex smiled. 'Yes, we'll be fine. We'll finish up and take ourselves to bed. I'm sure Dad will be fine in the morning.'

Smiling sadly at this statement, she reached down and gave him a big hug. 'Enjoy your day tomorrow; I'll see you for your horse riding adventure on Wednesday.'

Once he'd seen her off, Alex re-joined his family at the table. He'd lost his appetite for the desserts but made an effort to keep his brother, who seemed oblivious to the tension in the air, company. He looked at his Dad who was staring off sullenly into space and, recognising that they were no longer registering on his radar, encouraged Ben to finish up. When Ben was scraping his bowl clean, he said, 'come on. Let's get this lot into the dishwasher and get ready for bed. I'll read you a story if you like?'

Ben, who was exhausted from the day's exploits, brooked no argument with the plan and the pair of them dutifully loaded the dishwasher and set it running before saying goodnight to their dad. They found Leonard had moved into the lounge and was strumming abstractly on his guitar. He looked up when they entered.

'Everything alright boys?' he asked automatically, not showing much interest.

'All good, Dad,' replied Alex. 'We're just going to bed. Do you need anything? Would you like a coffee?' he asked pointedly.

Glancing at the wine bottle that had travelled into the lounge with him, Leonard declared, 'no, you're all right, son, I'm fine. Get yourselves settled and I will come up and say goodnight in a bit.'

As they were brushing their teeth at the sink, Ben paused, mouth foaming, and effused, 'I really like Isabella. I wish she was our mum. That Luka is very lucky; imagine having a mum that can cook like that'

'I like her, too,' noted Alex thoughtfully, looking at his brother's reflection in the ornate mirror. 'And I know what you mean; the food she made was lovely. I can't remember the last time mum was in the kitchen for anything other than a coffee.'

'It's a shame we can't have two mums, like Adrian. He has his real mum and when his dad got remarried, he got another one. He gets two holidays, two Christmases and everything!' Ben reported emphatically, spitting noisily and messily into the sink.

Alex stopped mid brush; the plan that had been hovering in his mind earlier that would mean they could spend more time with Isy, suddenly took on a more serious edge.

'Did you notice the way Dad was looking at her earlier?' he asked his brother. 'He had a very strange look on his face. I think he might like her,' he added hopefully.

Ben, worried about not being in the loop, thought for a moment. 'You could be right, I guess. But I'm pretty sure she doesn't like him. He's been very mean to her. She doesn't know he gets grumpy sometimes, but if you wait it out he's all alright again, isn't he?' he looked earnestly at Alex.

Knowing Ben didn't always understand their father's 'mood swings', he rushed to reassure him. 'Our Dad is the best,' he maintained, placing his hand on his brother's shoulder, 'don't you forget that. It's Detective Inspector Fierce that mucks everything up and makes him sad. But I think having someone like Isabella to cheer him up would be a good thing. We need to try and get them to spend more time together so she can realise he isn't so bad most of the time!'

Beaming at the idea of being involved in a nefarious plan, especially one that involved spending more time with Isy and possibly cheering his Dad up at the same time, Ben nodded so hard he bumped his chin on the sink, causing him to wince but, determined not to cry, he carried on smiling bravely as Alex explained his idea.

BEYOND THE SEA

The following day dawned bright and sunny yet again, the morning's sun's rays streaming cruelly through the patio doors of the villa, once again causing Leonard to flinch in his sleep, before muttering and finally, carefully, venture opening one sticky eye. He took in his location, on the sofa yet again, and took in the empty wine bottle and the spilled glass on the coffee table. The deep red stain it had left across the unvarnished wood looking vaguely like a Rorschach test and acting as a sharp reminder of his lapse last night.

Groaning, he forced his body upright, and when the world finally stopped spinning, he searched for his phone to check the time. Eventually finding it lodged under the cushion that had served as his pillow for the night, he swiped the screen to life. Heart sinking, he saw he'd missed 10 messages and 28 calls from Angelica. Not able to deal with his agents' hysteria just yet, he threw the phone to one side, gingerly got to his feet and shuffled into the kitchen for some much needed coffee.

Managing to insert the pod after several shaky attempts, he hit the button and the noise of the machine pumping out its life giving nectar brought the boys running downstairs. They had been waiting for him to wake up for hours, desperate to set in motion the plan they had hatched last night, but knowing better than to wake him before he was ready. Throwing each other knowing glances, they chorused cheerfully, 'Morning Dad,' oblivious to the wince that it inspired.

'What are we going to do today?' inquired Alex, taking charge, and setting their plan into motion, all the while taking in his father's dishevelled appearance, bleary eyes, and general look of displeasure at being alive.

'Ah, well, I think we'll just have a quiet one, eh?' muttered Leonard, fighting down the overwhelming, impending urge to vomit. 'Boys at home, having a good time and all that,' he added pathetically, guilt riding in waves in symphony with his nausea that was wracking his body with a familiar rhythm.

He felt dreadful, and not just physically, he only had one precious week with his sons and he was wasting it getting wasted. He couldn't believe he had let himself, and them, down again and trying not to shout at the coffee machine for its lack of speed, forced a grin on his face and focused on his sons.

Alex nudged his brother sharply in the ribs, who immediately announced, in the voice of an automaton. 'I would like to do more snorkelling,' and looked proudly at Alex, who nodded slightly.

Leonard, totally oblivious to the play being presented to him, in his effort to focus on the conversation, responded, 'well we can do that in the pool. It'll be good practice for you.' The idea of having to do anything so grown up as getting in the car right now unimaginable, he could barely support his own weight, let alone control a car. He knew from experience it would be awhile before he could function and wanted to keep them occupied until that happened.

Ben, not knowing how to proceed, looked desperately at Alex, who hypothesized, 'we can't snorkel in the pool Dad, there's nothing to see!' in a desperate attempt to move 'The Plan' forward.

Leaning against the wooden work surface for support, Leonard downed his coffee in one and angrily banged his cup on the counter 'why do these infernal machines give you such small doses!' he demanded to the world at large. Seeing that it might be a little soon for their plan to be accepted, Alex took his dad by the hand and led him gently back to the sofa.

'Just sit here, Dad; I'll get you some more coffee.'

Leaving Leonard slumped angrily; staring off at nothing in particular on the sofa, Alex hot footed it back into the kitchen where Ben was trying ineffectually to insert another pod into the machine.

'I think he needs a few more of these before we mention going to that beach,' whispered the small boy warily. 'He doesn't look happy.'

Taking over the coffee production, Alex assured 'Don't worry Ben, we've got this. Operation New Mum will be underway soon. We really need to get some food into him, get the ham and cheeses and stuff from the fridge. I'll make him breakfast and then we can convince him that we need to go to Zlatni Rat,' he said, carefully pronouncing the name that he had memorised the night before. Soon both boys were busy and did a reasonable job of pulling together a breakfast for their father and themselves setting the table outside.

'Come on, Dad' called Ben when they were ready and although it was extremely high on the list of things Leonard did not want to do right now, he forced himself to his feet and went to join the boys at the table.

Isabella, despite not having a hangover, felt equally bleary when Luka jumped on her that morning shouting, 'are we going swimming today? You said we were going swimming today! It's your day off. We're going swimmmmmming' very loudly and repeatedly until she got out of bed.

A second night of tossing and turning, the various moments of enthrallment followed by moments of hatred with Leonard running endlessly through her brain until she wanted to bang it against the wall to make it stop. She had finally fallen into an exhausted slumber just as the sun started to rise, which was, she realised, looking at her phone, about an hour and a half ago.

'Ok, Ok' she grinned at Luka, embracing his small

frame in a welcome hug 'I'm moving. How about pancakes for breakfast?' she asked, more chirpily than she felt, in an effort to distract both of them. At least it was her day off and she wouldn't have to deal with that stupid man today, unless he did something else ridiculous and needed rescuing again, which she desperately hoped he wouldn't. A day without him blowing hot and cold, confusing her body and her mind, was just what she needed. Smiling at Luka as she pulled on her robe and walked through to the kitchen to mix up the batter for pancakes, imagining the day ahead she found herself singing a song.

Unfortunately, it dawned on her that it was the one she had heard last night, the one that Leonard had been singing so sweetly. As soon as she realised what she was doing, her mouth clamped shut and, keeping it firmly closed, she flicked on her speaker and selected her favourite 'happy' playlist from Spotify on her phone. She refused to let that silly man interfere with her day.

After the last drops of maple syrup had been wiped from their plates, she and Luka agreed on the couple of small household jobs that needed to be done before the grand 'day off' could commence. Hers, as ever, mostly involved laundry and cleaning, but Luka was set the task of designing a card for his grandfather whose birthday it was tomorrow. Knowing her son would spend painstaking hours over the card if left to his own devices, she set a time limit, for her benefit as much as his. It was easy to get lost in outstanding jobs and she refused to spend her whole day off playing catch up.

As she hung out the freshly washed bedding on the line, the thought of the two boys at the villa kept popping into her mind. She felt oddly responsible for them despite barely knowing them. Shrugging off that thought and focusing on her own son, she quickly finished up the jobs she wanted to do and went into Luka's bedroom to see how he was getting on with his art project.

Beaming at her, he proudly showed her the drawing he had made of his grandpa fishing, his favourite pastime, on the front of the card he had created, and asked if he should add glitter to it. Knowing how liberal her son was with glue and glitter, she interjected hopefully, 'you know what, Luka, it's pretty perfect right now, and I don't think it needs glitter.'

Her son, basking in the glow of her praise, looked at his creation for a moment and then nodded his consent 'I think you're right mamma, can we go to Zlatni Rat now?'

Delighted that he had conceded so easily, Isabella was more than happy to concur and smiling at him chirped, 'come on then, let's get going.' Hastily texting Sandy to let her know where they would be today if she wanted to join them, Isabella collected up their ever ready beach bag from beside the front door, adding a fresh change of clothes for Luka just in case, and bundled her son into the car ready for their day together.

When they arrived at the beach, it was sparsely populated. Just a few die hard tourists, determined to get a tan and some local families making the most of the late summer heatwave that Croatia was experiencing. Happy to see that their usual sunbeds were available in front of their favourite beach bar they soon had themselves organised. Years of habit coming into play as they silently disrobed, automatically standing in front of one another to apply sun lotion and were swimming along the reefs, masks firmly in the water, in no time.

All thoughts of Leonard forgotten, Isabella revelled in the freedom she felt when swimming in the sea. The fact she could share this with Luka doubled the pleasure she felt and time disappeared as they explored the familiar reefs along the bay. It was only when her stomach started growling she realised it must be nearly lunchtime and she waved at Luka and pointed back towards the way they had swam to let him know it was time for a pit stop.

When she stood up in the shallows, shaking her hair and removing her mask it came as a cold, hard slap across the face, to discover Sandy, firmly ensconced at one of the tables at their bar, gaily talking to Leonard and his sons, the boys happily eating chips, their faces smeared with ketchup.

Stopping in her tracks as she was making her way out of the sea, she let out an unaccustomed expletive. 'Bloody hell,' she muttered 'just what I don't need.' Torn between not wanting to see Leonard and not wanting to leave Sandy alone with him. God knows what she would say. She hesitated on the edge of the water. Just then Ben looked up and saw her and shouted loudly, 'hello Isy!' which made the decision for her.

Walking across to where they were seated, she quickly picked up her towel as she passed the sunbeds and wrapped it firmly around her body, she didn't want Leonard gawking at her. Stopping briefly to help Luka with his, she then closed the distance between them and plastered a smile on her face.

'What are you doing here?' she challenged as nonchalantly as she could to Leonard and then, realising how rude that sounded, added, 'I thought you were spending the day at the villa?'

Leonard, who'd been entranced by the vision of her emerging from the water and the droplets running down the voluptuous curves of her body before they were so swiftly hidden beneath a towel, took a long moment to respond.

'Ah, well, it seems like my boys had other ideas' he shrugged his shoulders apologetically, as if he wasn't allowed to deviate from her itinerary. 'They enjoyed the snorkelling so much yesterday they decided we should do some more today and they remembered you'd mentioned that this beach was great for snorkelling. I hope we are not interfering with your day off?'

Remembering that she had indeed mentioned that this beach was great for snorkelling and knowing that she didn't have much choice babbled gaily 'no it's fine, the more the merrier' and ignoring the smirking coming from Sandy, introduced Luka to the other boys. As is the way with small boys worldwide, they soon got over their initial shyness and were competitively racing up and down the beach in a never ending game of tag.

'Soooo' trilled Sandy into the silence that had fallen between the adults on the boy's departure, 'I think it's beer O'clock, don't you?'

Leonard leapt on the opportunity to collect his thoughts and stood up immediately; 'I'll get them,' he exclaimed and without waiting to hear their response, walked over to the bar to place the order.

'Well, this is a turn up for the books,' exclaimed Sandy happily 'I get to meet the lovely Leonard and I get to watch you squirm in embarrassment at the same time!'

'What have you been saying to him?' Isabella demanded abruptly, worried that her friend may have been talking about her.

'Don't you worry, I didn't say anything about your feelings for him,' she mocked teasingly.

'I do not have feelings for him, he's a jerk' replied Isabella angrily, trying to pull up a small corner of her towel to her hair without revealing anything.

'Well, that "jerk" has totally got the hots for you,' offered Sandy slyly. 'as soon as he realised I knew you, he couldn't stop talking about you. And when you came out of the sea, he couldn't take his eyes off you. He was all agog.' She giggled, then tried to silence it as she saw Leonard approaching the table, holding a tray with three beers balanced precariously on it.

Having safely delivered them without mishap, he sat down and he raised his glass aloft 'what shall we drink to?' he enquired, looking from one to the other, trying not to stare at Isabella.

'How about love?' speculated Sandy, following suit, holding out her glass, her eyes twinkling with mischievousness.

'How about happy days' replied Isabella firmly, unable to think of anything else and clinking her glass against theirs firmly, deciding the toast, before taking a huge swig from her beer to cover her embarrassment.

☼

Back in London, Angelica, becoming increasingly frustrated at Leonard's lack of communication and being bombarded daily with emails from Sublime Retreats as to the whereabouts of the photos promised for their Instagram page, decided she would have to take action. She was pretty sure Leonard's attempts at photography would be halfhearted at best, if he indeed remembered at all, and the week was passing quickly.

Calling on an old contact who owed her a few favours, she explained what she needed and gave the photographer carte blanche with his budget to travel out to Croatia and save her promotional skin. Satisfied that she'd done what she could to salvage that particular farce, she decided to add a little fuel to the fire surrounding Rennie's wedding and nuptial bliss.

Tapping on the contacts on her phone, she found the number of the reporter who had been making the most of the story, giving daily updates on the happy couple's cavorting in the Bahamas alongside plenty of photos of Rennie in various, barely there bikinis.

'Morning, Dave,' she drawled when he answered, 'just wanted to thank you for all the coverage you've been giving Rennie.

A deep, throaty laugh that paid more than a passing nod to a 40 a day cigarette habit came down the line.

'Not exactly a problem,' responded the newshound, coughing into the receiver 'she's top of the pops as far as my readers are concerned. I'd be a fool not to make the most of it!'

Nodding pointlessly back in her office, Angelica's tone took on an extra layer of oily undercurrent 'I am surprised you haven't been following up on the other side of the story though' she added, pausing to let this sink in.

Ears pricking up on the other side of the world, Dave took a long draw from his cigarette before responding, 'Tell me,' he demanded without preamble.

'Well, far be it from me to break a confidence,' Angelica continued smoothly, lying through her well-kept teeth 'but what if I was to tell you that a certain detective was heartbroken at the moment and off on holiday, licking his wounds?' she enquired seductively.

'I would say that was extremely interesting,' the hack replied 'I would only wonder where such a person would go when they were feeling like that. Where do you think they would go, Angelica?'

'Well, if I was to hazard a guess, I would say somewhere fairly remote, a small island somewhere maybe, like Brač?'

'Understood' replied Dave before cutting the call and speed dialling a photographer friend of his.

Satisfied with her morning's work, she collected her things together and walked out of the office. She was meeting a delicious new talent at The Wolseley for lunch, who she wanted to add to her stable. The thrill of that particular chase combining with her love of the lobster and caviar eggs served in the fabulous art deco restaurant put her in extremely good humour and she smiled at Amanda, her PA on the way out, calling 'I'm off for lunch' gaily and leaving the poor woman feeling slightly perturbed.

Back at the beach the atmosphere had relaxed a great deal, the three adults eventually falling into easy conversation as the boys played happily on the beach, stopping by only occasionally to grab a drink or show of a particularly interested pebble they'd found, a small pile of which was now building up in a precarious pile on the table.

'So Leonard' babbled Sandy easily, chatting away now she had got over her initial starstruckness and had a second beer 'how are you enjoying Brač?'

'I absolutely love it,' he replied easily, glancing up as a laughing Ben ran by the table. 'It's so beautiful here and it's wonderful to be with my sons for a whole week,' he added wistfully 'we are all definitely having the best holiday of our lives. I wish it wasn't going by so quickly!'

Smiling with pride at a job well done, Isabella advised gently, 'you're only halfway through you know; don't wish your life away Leo' causing him to look at her sharply as he realised that was pretty much what he'd been doing with his life these last couple of years and that coming from her, "Leo" didn't sound quite so bad.

As their gaze lengthened, their eyes locked in an unbreakable gaze, Sandy became increasingly aware she was the third wheel in this particular group and, casting around for topics, asked brightly, 'so what have you got planned for tomorrow?' to break the spell.

Leonard looked briefly dazed as his attention snapped back unwillingly to the present and he looked inquiringly at Isy, as he had no idea what he was supposed to be doing tomorrow.

Taking her cue, Isabella answered for him, 'tomorrow he's taking the boys horse riding in the morning' she said 'I'm going to show them the way, I don't want them getting lost' she added causing the two of them to share a knowing look, that of a private joke, making Sandy feel more out of place.

'Well, as you're going to be there, you should go for a ride,' smirked Sandy a little cruelly, knowing full well her friend had never been horse riding in her life and was extremely wary of horses.

Throwing an angry glance at Sandy, Isabella snapped, 'oh I'm sure Leonard wants to enjoy time alone with his boys.'

'Oh, please come with us,' exclaimed Alex, who had

arrived with his brother unnoticed behind her 'we'd love it if you came with us, wouldn't we, Ben?'

'Oh gosh yes,' replied the boy enthusiastically nodding 'it would make the whole day perfect if you came too. You could bring Luka'

Torn between not wanting to disappoint the boys and not wanting to get on a large, seemingly uncontrollable, mad eyed looking beast of an animal she stalled 'well Luka is spending the day with his grandfather, it's his birthday tomorrow, they are going fishing and then I'm joining them for a party in the afternoon' she backtracked, hoping this would be the end of it and put paid to Sandy's little plot.

Sandy, not to be beaten, smiled sweetly 'Well that gives you no excuse to go out riding with them in the morning then, does it?' and smirked at her friend's obvious discomfort.

Knowing exactly what Sandy was up to a flash of anger and bravado swept through her 'you know what, I think I will go' she proclaimed 'it will be fun' she added with a complete lack of conviction trying to smile at them and convince herself at the same time.

'Hooray' shouted Leonard's sons in unison, causing everyone to laugh, albeit somewhat reservedly in Isabella's case. 'Dad, don't forget to take some photos,' said Alex dutifully, finally remembering his task. Leonard started guiltily and, thinking of the missed calls from his agent, stood up 'well remembered, Alex. Let's get a shot of us here to send in. I'm sure they would like that.'

Quick as a flash, Sandy jumped up. 'I'll take it, you

guys group together there with Isy. I think Sublime Retreats would love to see their concierge being so involved in her guests' holiday!' Unable to refute that claim, Isabella forced a smile through her clenched teeth as Ben climbed on her lap and Leonard and Alex moved in either side of her for the shot.

'Put your arms around her boys,' called out Sandy, thoroughly enjoying herself at this point, and snapped away happily when they did. Isabella, trying to ignore the weight of Leonard's arm draped casually across her shoulder, kept what she hoped looked like a genuine smile on her face and was thankful she didn't have an Instagram account and would never have to see the result.

Luka, who'd up till now been absorbed in a game of skipping stones across the languid, turquoise waters, came bouncing up and demanded to join in the photo shoot. Ben insisted on digging his camera out of his small bag and getting Sandy to take another picture. Looking down at the camera Sandy asked, 'this is your last shot Ben. Are you sure you want to use it now?'

Obviously struggling with not wanting to use it up, yet wanting to capture this moment, he took a long time before answering 'it's ok, go for it!' so she obliged, making sure to take a good one for him.

'Right people', she announced walking back up to the table and handing the camera back to the eager boy, 'I'm afraid I'll have to love you and leave you' she announced to the group at large 'I have to go home and get ready for work.' Sandy always liked to look her best for work as she ran the front of house, so dolled up every night to look glam for her customers.

Watching her friend leave, Isabella wasn't sure what to do next. She didn't want to spoil her sons fun, and they certainly hadn't done enough swimming yet today for either of them to be satisfied so hoping to extract them from the situation, stood up, firmly pulling her towel back around her now dry body and said 'come on Luka, it's time for us to go snorkelling again.'

She knew as soon as the words were out of her mouth it was the wrong thing to say and inevitably Leonard's boys leapt on the suggestion and Alex cried 'Yes, come on Dad, we haven't been in the sea yet!' and started tugging at his arm in an effort to get him to move. Luka, thrilled at the prospect of swimming with his new friends, shouted, 'come on, let's get our masks!' and ran to the sunbeds followed by his new friends.

Looking extremely awkward, Leonard muttered, 'it looks like you've been roped in, sorry' as he stood up and pulled some money out of his pocket to pay the bar bill. 'I can take them somewhere else if you prefer?'

'Don't be silly, you're here now' snapped Isy, then realising how harsh she had sounded continued 'anyway, I think we'd have world war three on our hands if we try to separate them now' she smiled at him then nodded across to where the boys were, standing in the shallows, masks already on, jumping up and down impatiently waiting for their parents to join them.

With a nod of acceptance, Leonard scooped up the beach bags and walked with Isabella over to where her snorkelling gear had been hastily thrown on her sunbed earlier. Eventually they were ready, and feeling very self-conscious, Isabella dropped her towel and ran to the water, wanting to submerge her body as quickly as possible.

'Come on boys, let's go that way' she called, pointing to the left side of the bay and sliding gracefully into the water she swam off. The boys plopped in behind her and started following along, much like a group of ducklings. Smiling into his mask at this thought, Leonard followed suit and was soon slipping easily through the languid waters, catching up with them in no time.

☼

To Isabella's surprise, they had a wonderful afternoon. Leonard was strangely easy company, and the boys got on so well they were all less demanding of their parents, happy to have someone new to show off to. A couple of hours later, when they had finally exhausted all the wonders to be found in the seabed of the bay, they finally dragged themselves out of the water and clustered round the sunbed, in various stages of undress, discussing the day's finds.

'Mine was best' insisted Ben, proudly clutching the dusty orange remains of the starfish he had found on the beach throughout the vigorous drying session Leonard had given him with a towel, and wouldn't even let go when his t-shirt was slipped awkwardly over his head.

Rubbing his hair with a towel, Leonard was feeling

much better. Today's activities had washed away the last of his hangover, and he was feeling buoyant.

'How about we all go and grab some dinner somewhere?' he threw out casually without even thinking about it, to a chorus of cheers from the boys. Glancing over at Isy, he saw she had stopped mid rummage in her bag where she was searching for a hair band and was looking rather startled, like a deer caught in the headlights.

Realising he may have stepped over a boundary, but not sure exactly which one, he hurried to make good. 'I'd like to thank you for all your hard work, Isabella. This whole holiday has been lovely, so far, despite my continued efforts to muck it up,' he smiled deprecatingly, 'and that's all down to your organisational skills.'

Feeling strangely put out that he'd pointed out her organisational skills rather than the wonderful afternoon they'd had together she said 'Oh that's not necessary' as she finally fished the errant band out of the recesses of her bag and skilfully twisted her hair into place. Satisfied that it was under control, she finally risked a glance at him. He was sitting on the sunbed now, looking so lost and forlorn and much like his boys who were perched beside him that she felt a pang of guilt at her glib reaction to what had obviously been an olive branch.

'But it's very kind of you to offer,' she added, hoping to soften the blow.

'But I'm hungry, Mum,' complained Luka 'I thought we were going to Auntie Sandy's for dinner?' Laughing, she bent down to put his shoes on 'You are always hungry, Luka, and I'm sure Leonard and the boys have better things to do,' causing the boy to pout his displeasure at this idea.

'Listen, Isabella,' answered Leonard seriously, watched closely by his sons 'I would really like us to do this.'

Feeling an unusual flutter in her stomach at the use of the word 'us', Isabella balanced on a precipice of indecision. She really wanted this day not to end, but on the other hand, she knew she should nip this emerging familiarity they were feeling in the bud, for her own sanity, if nothing else.

'Please can we come with you to Sandy's restaurant?' said Alex plaintively, standing up to emphasize his plea.

The boys' genuine desire pushed her over the precipice and, abandoning common sense completely, Isabella laughed as she felt a surge of excitement. 'I guess it won't hurt for us to have dinner there together,' although she knew Sandy's reaction when they walked in together would be worth anything this night was going to cost her.

The restaurant was perched on the side of the mountain above Bol with sweeping views down across the bay, with the twinkling lights of Hvar visible in the distance. Pulling her car up at the side of the road, Isabella glanced in her rear-view mirror and saw the distinctive green Karl pulling in behind her. Checking her reflection, she smiled, there was no denying the sparkle in her eyes.

'Come on, Mum,' demanded Luka, impatiently straining against the straps of his seat in the back. Prompted into action, she got herself and her son out of the car and stood waiting for the other family to join her before they walked over to the entrance.

As they walked in, Sandy, who had been barking orders at a beleaguered waitress with her back to them, spun around with a smile in place to greet her guests. The look on her face when she registered who had just come in was priceless. Swiftly collecting her wits she smoothed down her already skin tight dress, a vivid red with more than a nod to the East, and smiled again before saying 'well look who we have here, how very nice to see you again Leonard, so soon' she added looking pointedly at Isabella.

Knowing there was nothing in this world that was going to stop the flow of insinuation and innuendoes from her friend this evening, Isabella relaxed into the moment and decided just to enjoy it for whatever it was.

'Hi Sandy, we were all a little hungry after our afternoon swimming so we thought we'd come and see you for some dinner,' she announced as if it was the most natural thing in the world to be having dinner with a famous TV star.

Taking her cue from Isabella, Sandy slipped into her work role and replied smoothly, 'well luckily we are quiet tonight and I have a lovely table out on the terrace for you' and unable to help herself 'it's very romantic' she continued before walking up the three wooden stairs that led to the terrace. Hiding her smile, Isabella gestured to the others to follow, and they made their way out onto the terrace, stopping for a moment to admire the incredible view it afforded.

As they took their places, the boys instinctively sitting themselves together at the end of the table nearest the balcony so they could look over the edge. Leonard and Isy were left to take the two chairs left facing each other.

As she sat, she glanced around. It had been a while since she'd been here, she realised, and Sandy and her husband had been working hard on renovating the place. It was indeed romantic, with low-level lighting and the candles flickering their magic glow on every table. There were just two other tables occupied on the terrace this evening, couples Isy noted, enjoying the atmosphere and lost in each other to the exclusion of what was going on around them. With a pang, Isabella realised she missed that, that feeling of being so immersed with someone else that nothing else mattered, even in a public place like this. Suddenly aware she was staring, she brought her thoughts back to the present and the enthusiastic chatter of the boys at the other end of the table.

Leonard, who'd been entranced by the sight of Isabella's face, lit up by the glow of the candle on the table, as she'd been sat staring off at the other diners, felt a sharp stab of emotion when he saw her warm smile at the kids when she returned her glance to them. She was such a genuinely loving person; he thought and found himself comparing her to Rennie. The contrast was striking and not in the pop star's favour.

Sandy returned to the table, baring menus for them and ready to take their drinks orders. After much deliberation, the boys decided inevitably on cokes, which left Leonard and Isabella to make their decision. After a few moments of them umming and ahhing and painful indecision, Sandy, aware that the restaurant was filling up, decided to speed things up and continue mixing things up a bit in the process.

'I think this calls for some champagne, don't you?' she declared, snapping her notebook decisively and deliberately just looking at Leonard, who gratefully jumped on the suggestion and nodded enthusiastically.

'Perfect,' he muttered and looked to Isy for confirmation. Still going with the flow of whatever the universe had in store for her that evening, she gave in easily and smiled brightly at the two of them 'why not' she responded simply.

An awkward silence fell between them when Sandy left to get their drinks, which he hastily tried to fill.

'So Isabella, what do you like to do when you are not looking after your guests so well?' he asked disarmingly. Smiling at him across the table 'well that takes up quite a lot of my time. Some of them are quite demanding' she replied with a small laugh to show that no there were no hard feelings. Smiling back in acknowledgement of this jest, he remained silent and waited for her to continue.

'I love gardening,' she admitted shyly. 'I spend as much time as I can in the garden, growing vegetables for Luka and I to eat,' she added, warming to her theme. 'It's very satisfying; cooking something you've grown and picked yourself.'

Leonard, who had absolutely no experience in this and was the opposite of green fingered, barely able to keep even his cactus alive. 'Well, it's very satisfying eating something you've cooked' in a desperate attempt to contribute.

'I'm glad you enjoyed the meal' she smiled as Sandy returned with an ice bucket, a bottle of Dom and two champagne flutes. Deftly twisting the bottle and releasing the cork, she poured the champagne with a flourish and placed the glasses in front of them. 'Enjoy!' she proclaimed 'I'll be back shortly to take your food orders' and, giving Isy a sly wink, walked back into the restaurant.

Glad for something to do, they both snatched up their menus and started to read. As is the way of choosing food, they soon started discussing the pros and cons of the meals on offer, Isabella happily explaining to Leonard what was involved in the various local dishes and both of them deciding to make the choice for their sons as it would be a lengthy process otherwise.

They opted for a selection of starters, along with some garlic bread and simple pasta dishes for the kids. For themselves Isabella recommended Lamb Peka, a personal favourite of hers with chunks of lamb, potatoes and vegetables traditionally slowly cooked in a wood fire oven, with wine, oil and herbs for a couple of hours.

Looking over the top of his champagne flute, Leonard smiled sweetly at Isabella. 'I think this deserves another toast?'

'I think you might be right' she smiled back at him, savouring the intimacy that had developed between them 'what do you think it should be?' she realised with a start that she was flirting and quickly added 'how about to the perfect end to our happy day?'

Leonard gave a nod, remembering her earlier toast, and chinked his glass carefully against hers. The rest of the evening passed with a mixture of good food, laughter, and easy conversation. Before she even realised he was paying the bill and they were gathering their, by now, tired children and making their way back to their cars.

'Hope to see you all again soon,' called Sandy as they walked out the door, and feeling so content Isabella didn't bother to rise to her friend's pointed comment, and just smiled knowingly at her.

As they reached the cars, Leonard, who had a sleepy Ben in his arms, paused and they stared at each other for a moment, unsure what to say, as the magic of the evening slid away like so much silk, cast aside.

'So, I guess we'll see you in the morning,' he hesitated, sounding uncertain.

Stepping into her work persona with an almost audible snap, Isabella smiled at him. 'Yes, of course,' she said whilst opening the rear door of her car to place an equally sleepy Luka into his car seat.

'I will be with you about 9, the riding is booked for 10 so that gives us plenty of time' she continued her voice sounding slightly muffled from the recesses of the backseat, strewn with toys, scraps of paper and other unidentifiable things that Leonard's OCD decided to ignore. Looking helplessly at her back as she battled with the fastenings, Leonard struggled to find the words to express how he was feeling.

'I really enjoyed today' he heard himself saying lamely, and kicked himself mentally for being so inept at expressing his feelings.

'I did too,' she responded as she finally clicked the belts into place and stood up. 'If you follow me down the hill, I will pull over by the turning for the villa so you know where to go,' she said brightly and walked around to the driver's door, effectively ending the potentially dangerous conversation that she felt brewing.

Alex, who had been watching this exchange with serious intent, smiled before saying 'come on Dad' and tugging on his father's sleeve before he could say anything else stupid and led the way back to their car.

As she sat behind the wheel, Isabella took a moment to compose herself, forcing the intoxicating bubbles building inside her down for the time being. There was plenty of time to dissect the day later. Glancing in the mirror to check that they were safely in their car and ready to follow, she started the engine and indicated to pull out, but not before she noticed the silly, huge grin on her glowing face.

CRAZY HORSES

Derek James, the freelance photographer, had laughed out loud when he received another call asking him to go to Croatia immediately after putting the phone down to Angelica. Having no qualms about the possible conflict of interest, he easily accepted both jobs and packed his bag. As the day dawned bright and clear, it found him camped in his hire car, a short way down from the villa, ready to move into place once he saw signs of activity.

He watched with interest as just before 9 a woman with a mass of curly hair drove past him and continued up to the villa. Pulling out his camera and zooming in as she pulled up in front of the building, he watched as she walked confidently up to the front door and pressed the bell on one side to announce her presence. His interest piqued even further a moment later when the door was opened by the young boy he knew to be Ben, the youngest Lupine brat, who broke into a huge, beaming smile on seeing her and threw himself into her waiting arms for a hug.

'Well, well, well, what do we have here then?' he muttered, snapping away rapidly until the door finally shut. With a sense that this job was going to turn out even more lucrative than he had originally envisioned, he happily settled down to wait to see what would come next.

Inside the villa, Isabella found Leonard in the kitchen, clearing away the last of the breakfast things and carefully wiping down the surfaces. She smiled when she thought of the disparity between this image and the character he played. Sandy had insisted she watch an episode of Fierce Conflicts and sent her a YouTube link, which, despite her best intentions, she had watched, and strangely enjoyed, although she was not going to admit that to Sandy.

But knowing now how the rest of the world saw this man and comparing it to the person she was getting to know, she was amazed at the difference between the two men. They couldn't be less alike if they tried. She was beginning to see that Leonard fell back into his character when he was uncomfortable or stressed, but underneath that was someone else, someone hiding from the world; it was as if he was frightened to show his true self.

'Good morning,' she called brightly and was rewarded with a wonderful smile that thrilled her down to her brightly painted toenails and halted her in her tracks.

'Isabella' he said simply and stood gazing at her stupidly. After a moment of basking in his goofy smile, she took control of pounding heart and the situation and asked, 'are you boys ready for today's adventure?'

'Uhm, yes, I think so,' he vacillated, seeming completely unsure, casting about for forgotten things.

'We are ready Dad!' insisted Alex. 'We've been ready for ages' he cried plaintively. And indeed both boys were standing, backpacks in place, patiently waiting for the grownups to get organised.

'Ah, ok son, let me just grab my wallet and things' and Leonard wandered off into the lounge to hunt for them. 'You seem a little distracted this morning,' she called after his retreating back.

'Dad was up all night pretty much,' voiced Alex as he helped Ben re-tie his shoes. 'He started writing his song again when we got home and he was still at it when we woke up!' he exclaimed in wonder at the fact someone could spend so long writing.

Leonard returned, waving the car keys at them and said, 'Alex suggested that as you are coming riding with us you may as well come in our car?' and looked at her hopefully.

Unable to think of a plausible reason why not, Isabella nodded her assent, and they made their way towards the door, but not before she noticed a look of triumph flash between the two boys which made her wonder if there was more behind the suggestion than common sense.

Derek sat up straight as they came out, his finger poised in anticipation. He had a tingling feeling this story was going to be a big one, and he didn't want to miss a moment. He was shortly rewarded with the sight of the unknown woman helping Leonard Lupine's sons into the back of his car and all of them laughing at some unheard joke. He snapped away, only putting the camera down when the car started to come down the drive. When they drove past a few moments later, they didn't pay any attention to the man in the hire car that seemed to be intently studying a map.

'So I hear you've been up all night writing?' Isy queried, taking the opportunity to study Leonard's profile as he concentrated on the road. 'Was it your song?'

'Yes, I've nearly got it done, I think. I felt inspired last night for some reason' he smiled happily and cast a quick glance at her before focusing back on the road.

Feeling she needed to add something, she murmured, 'I hope I get to hear it before you leave.' His face fell for a moment and he seemed to be into deep thought for a few miles until Isy observed, 'we need the next turning on the left, the stables are just up there.'

Following her directions, a short while later they were pulling up outside a low level building, covered in climbing roses and as they climbed out of the car the age old, familiar scent of horses wafted over him and he was surprised at how bright the memories were that it evoked.

Jumping nervously at a distant whinny, Isabella asked 'have you ridden before?' over the roof of the car as he stood there smelling the slightly rancid air with apparent enjoyment.

'Not since I was a boy,' he gushed enthusiastically. 'I'm looking forward to this!' and took his son's hands and started to walk towards the woman who had come out at the sound of their car pulling up. 'Come on Isy' she muttered 'you can do this girl' cheering herself on, in an effort to stop her knees knocking, and she hadn't even seen a horse yet!

The girl who came out to meet them introduced herself as Anneke, and bore all the trademarks of a healthy outdoor lifestyle. Long-limbed, young and glowing with ruddy health, her thick hair in a long plait down her back, she explained she was a student working here on an exchange scheme and by the looks of it, loving every minute. She spent a moment explaining a little about the background of the stables and the fact that all the horses were rescue's, lovingly brought back to trusting humans with hours of patient work, until they were ready to earn their keep and enjoy the rest of their lives in this beautiful place.

Leading them around the back of the pretty, well-kept building to where the stables where things became a lot more functional. The well-tended, tidy garden of the front was replaced with a towering pile of hay bales waiting to be moved, a stack of metal buckets and a little further on was a mountain of the source of that distinctive smell.

She walked them past all of these, stopping at the tack room with them to fit their helmets, before leading them to the arena at the far end where five horses of various sizes and shades stood patiently waiting, idly flicking their tails at the flies buzzing around them and munching on the odd patches of grass they found on the barren ground.

'Here are our rides for today,' Anneke announced grandly 'these beauties are the stars of our stables and our longest serving guests, except for Sparky, right on the end there,' she pointed at a skittish looking white horse at the end of the line-up. 'He came to us last year from Slovenia and has been amazing in his turn-around, from a nervous, browbeaten animal to the happy, relaxed boy you see today. I think he may be part Lipizzaner,' she added proudly.

'They're the ones that dance, aren't they?' asked Leonard, surprising everyone.

'Yes, they are,' the girl replied 'and they turn white as they get older' she continued as the horse in question started to jink around, almost on tiptoes, his eyes rolling back in his head and nostrils flaring at the newcomers.

Positioned in the bushes taking shots of the group getting ready to mount, Derek took a moment to glance at the stables information that he'd quickly pulled up on his phone. They had two routes mapped out, one of which was for experienced riders, so he took a gamble that this mob would be taking the novice trail, as it was called. Let's face it, Leonard wasn't exactly famous for his outdoor skills, just his indoor at a bar skills, so it was unlikely they would be galloping off on the expert trail.

Checking the route of obvious spots where he could lurk he saw an ideal place just by the edge of the beach which was part of the walk, which according to Google maps had a small thicket of trees at the far end that he could hide in. Happy with the pictures he had so far, he trotted back to his car to make his way to the beach ahead of them.

With a sinking feeling, as she watched Anneke help the two boys onto the smaller horses, Isabella knew without a shadow of a doubt which four-legged beast was going to be hers. Leonard hoisted his lanky frame easily onto the back of the large brown mare he had been allotted with a grace he had so far shown no signs of and Isabella steeled herself for her turn.

Inevitably, Anneke took the halter of Sparky firmly in her right hand and waved Isy over with her other. 'Come, let's get you on, then we can be off,' she remarked, as if this was the most natural thing in the world. Hesitating for just a beat, Isabella tried to project confidence as she strode over to the horse, but the student obviously sensed her trepidation.

'Here, she said, pulling his nose towards her, why don't you say hi?'

Tentatively putting out her hand, Isabella stroked Sparky nervously for a moment, jumping a little as he investigated her pockets for the possibility of hidden treats. After a moment, she felt a little calmer and Anneke smiled at her and enquired 'ready?' to which she nodded and got in place to put her foot in the stirrup the way she had seen Leonard do it.

She eventually managed to haul her body on and wriggle into place, with none of the ease and grace that Leonard had shown, but determined not to let him and the boys see how uncomfortable she felt right now, she forced a grin onto her face as she looked around at them.

Checking she was all set, tightening stirrups with practiced ease, Anneke then jumped onto her horse lightly, proving practice did make perfect Isy thought with a grimace, and with a loud click of her tongue and a slight pressure on the reigns she turned her ride around and led them slowly towards the open gate at the end of the arena. They soon found themselves walking sedately down a well-trodden path through the trees, and Isy began to relax. The two boys were slightly ahead of her and thrilled with the whole thing, calling eagerly to each other and continually patting the neck of their horses as if in disbelief that they were actually there.

As they meandered along Isabella began to think that she'd been stupid all these years, she wasn't sure where her irrational fear of horses had come from, probably some imagined childhood trauma, but she was actually beginning to enjoy the feel of being perched up high and the slightly uncomfortable rhythm of Sparky's gait.

As she caught sight of the sea twinkling in the distance, she was idly thinking that she should organise to bring Luka one day when a shot rang out in the distance, causing Sparky to prance nervously on the spot. Anneke at the front of the column pulled up, forcing the three boys to stop, and called back to her, 'it's ok, just reassure him.'

Not sure how one did that, Isabella leant forward,

one foot slipping out of its stirrup as she bent down close to his neck, stroking him and making soothing noises. It seemed to be working as he settled down after a few minutes and Isy looked up and called to Anneke 'I think he's ok now' just as a second shot sounded, much closer this time.

Sparky decided that this was just too much and took off like a bullet himself, with Isabella bouncing uncontrollably in the saddle, desperately trying to rein him in and get her errant foot back in place at the same time.

'Pull on the reins,' Anneke called needlessly as the white flash forced its way past her, increasing speed as the other horses stumbled to get out of his way. Throwing a glance behind him to check his sons were ok, Leonard called 'stay with the boys' to the girl before kicking his mare into action and high tailing after Isy without a second thought.

Despite his fear, Sparky was following the path he knew best, and was soon cantering down towards the beach with Isabella clinging on for dear life, unable to do anything but pray that the universe would step in and save her, as her riding hat came loose and eventually bounced off to one side. As her uncontrollable mount hit the sand, he unbelievably seemed to pick speed and Isy closed her eyes, only to open them a moment later when she heard a voice calling to her.

Risking a glance over her shoulder, she saw Leonard bearing down on them at high speed, catching them up every pounding step. Before she knew what was happening, he was grabbing the reins of the terrified horse and pulling him gradually to a halt with his own. Once the horses finally stopped, he jumped off, throwing the reins over the saddle and held up his arms to a by now sobbing Isy, who slid down into them gratefully.

'It's ok, it's ok' he murmured like a soft mantra into her hair. When the sobbing died down he murmured gently, 'are you OK?' and she finally looked up at him with such a look on her face that he couldn't resist the urge and he kissed her. The world stopped turning for a moment. Isabella's incredible fear of the last few minutes replaced a remarkable feeling of rightness and her head started to spin for entirely different reasons as the kiss lengthened, sparked into something more serious.

They only pulled apart when they eventually became aware of the clinking of horse tack and looked up to see the others staring at them in amazement, the two boys grinning like mad. Alex looked over at his brother and gloated smugly, 'I told you so' before resuming an innocent expression.

Derek, perfectly placed at the end of the beach, had caught the whole gripping rescue on camera and was practically wetting himself with excitement as he took shots of the kiss, which would cause the female half of the British population to swoon on the spot. He felt like snogging the grumpy TV star himself, he'd provided him was such an amazing story.

He carried on snapping as the other three riders got down from their horses, the woman from the stables going straight to the deviant horse and taking his reins but the two boys went and wrapped their arms around the couple in a group hug that was sure to make headline news.

The group made their way back to the stables, Anneke leading a now complacent Sparky and Isabella held securely in front of Leonard on his horse. Isabella's mind was in turmoil. She couldn't work out which was more shocking, the bolting horse or the kiss and the fact that she was now ensconced in the arms of a man who she didn't think she liked.

On reflection, she decided it was the kiss. She'd always known horses were one step shy of crazy and today had proved it. But she couldn't deny her reaction to the kiss, or how comfortable she felt securely wrapped in his arms, despite being on yet another horse. It was wondrous yet terrifying at the same time and she couldn't let herself think what this could mean and just relaxed back into the warmth of his chest.

When they reached the safety of the stables and everyone had dismounted, Anneke was unable to apologise enough for Sparky's behaviour. 'He never does that, I'm so sorry Isabella, I don't know what to say' the poor girl looked so distraught; she was nearly in tears, that Isabella felt sorry for her.

'It's not your fault Anneke, or Sparky's' she added begrudgingly 'it was those stupid hunters, they should know better.'

Still apologising profusely, Anneke walked with them as they made their way back to the car and said her remorseful goodbyes.

☼

On the ride back, the children chattered happily about the day's adventure, but in the front of the car there was a strained silence. Both of them only nodding or grunting in response to the boy's comments, both lost in their own thoughts at what had happened and unsure how to proceed. It wasn't something you could ignore, but where the hell did they go now?

Back at the villa, Leonard asked if she would like tea or coffee to settle her nerves before she had to drive home. They were standing in the lounge, the boys having raced off to get their swimming trunks on, seeming unconcerned about what had happened and assuming in their naïve way that operation 'new mum' was now complete.

'I won't stop,' gabbled Isabella, glancing at the time 'I really have to get to Ivan's birthday Party, I promised Anna I would help with the cooking...' she trailed off.

'Listen,' started Leonard, 'about today, what happened you know with the...'

'Let's not talk about that now' interrupted Isabella abruptly, not sure yet of her own feelings, let alone being able to discuss them.

'How about tomorrow?' Leonard asked hopefully.

'Tomorrow you are booked to go to Hvar on the boat,' she reminded him, secretly glad at another day's reprieve before having to face the situation.

'Why don't you come with us?' he asked suddenly 'bring Luka, the boys would love it.'

'I'm not sure' she hesitated, although the idea was very appealing on so many levels. Yes, she wanted to spend the day with him, but no, she definitely did not want to talk about what was happening between them.

Understanding in a flash where her hesitation was coming from and not wanting it to stop them spending time together, he maintained thoughtfully, 'Look, it's just a day. We don't have to talk about the... you know. Let's just have some fun together in Hvar and worry about anything else later.'

Smiling at this "get out of jail free card," that would allow her to enjoy another day with him without having to think too seriously about it, she nodded and announced, 'you're on! Luka will love it. He loves going on boats and he really enjoyed the other day with your two. It will be fun.'

He walked her back outside to her car where there was an awkward pause, as neither of them knew the etiquette now. Yes, they'd kissed, and what a kiss it had been, but what were they? Friends, concierge and guest, something more? Leonard bent down to kiss her cheek just as she stooped to get in the car and he ended up with a mouthful of hair. Choosing to ignore this, Isabella smiled at him from the sanctuary of the driver's seat and said, 'I'll see you tomorrow morning, 7.15 bright and early for the 8 o'clock boat' as she started her engine.

Standing on the drive, lost in thought for some time after her car had disappeared, Leonard was brought back to the present by the calls from his sons to go and join them in the pool. Scratching his head trying to dislodge the memory of that kiss and the afterglow it had left, he made his way back inside and, in an effort to join in the boys' glee, he got his trunks on.

☼

When Isabella arrived at Anna and Ivan's cottage she had no recollection of the journey there. She'd been so lost in thought that she must have been on automatic pilot and she thanked the stars that she had arrived safely. Finding Anna in the kitchen, Luka and his grandfather had not yet returned from their fishing trip, she soon lost herself in the food preparations and idle chatter, thankful for the distraction.

Never one to miss a party, Sandy arrived a short while later and although she immediately noticed her friends dreamy eyed stares and vague preoccupation, it was a good hour later before she could pull her to one side to find out what was going on. As they stood on the terrace, looking back inside at the milling around the food laden table as Ivan's friends and family made the most of the occasion, Sandy asked casually 'so, spill the beans. How was horse riding with Luscious Leonard?'

Taking a large gulp of the home made white wine in her glass; Isabella strove for words to describe the events of this morning.

'Well first off, I was right in my thinking, horses are completely mad and dangerous' she replied with a grimace 'Sparky' she added derisively 'decided to go cantering off with me barely holding on, it was terrifying!'

'Oh my god! I'm sorry, what happened exclaimed Sandy, instantly chagrined at her insistence that Isy joined the riding session.

'Well if it wasn't for Leonard coming to the rescue I don't know what would have happened. I'd probably be still going round the island right now if it wasn't for him.'

Sensing her friend wasn't telling her everything Sandy turned a beady eye on her 'so, tell me more?' and arched a knowing eyebrow at Isabella, who had the good grace to blush. Feeling the heat rising in her face she flapped ineffectually with her hand but could no more stop the colour from infusing her face than she could the smile that accompanied it.

'We kissed' she announced simply, watching as Sandy spat out a mouthful of wine and grabbed a paper napkin from a nearby table in an effort to dab at the damp stains on her dress.

'Well don't leave me hanging, tell me everything' she demanded, making the stain on her dress worse as the colour started to seep out of the napkin she was using. Laughing at the avid expression on Sandy's face she found she was more than happy to share what had happened with someone, it had been on the tip of her tongue all afternoon without a channel of release and now, finding its audience it leapt from her mouth in a stream of consciousness that left her gasping for breath when she finished.

'Wow' approved Sandy looking at her friend askew 'you only went and did it, you only went and snogged the luscious one!' Sandy felt a little discombobulated; she was usually the one regaling her friend with such exploits, as Isy looked on slightly disapprovingly, although Sandy was sure she enjoyed the vicarious involvement in her love life.

'So, what happens now? When are you going to see him again?'

'Well we are going to Hvar together tomorrow, with the boys' she added hastily as if this made it more right and proper, casting them in the role of chaperones, still not realising that they had other plans with regards to their parents.

'So is this it, is it official, is he your "boyfriend"' Sandy replied much in the way of a schoolyard chant.

Isabella laughed at her tone and replied 'I have no idea what it means; he wanted us to talk when we got back to the villa but I put him off. I need to get my head straight, if that's possible, and work out my feelings. I really don't know where I'm at with this at the moment, It might be just that he's the first man that's paid me any attention since I've been back here that's making my head spin.'

Knowing full well that her friend continually received admiring glances and had seen numerous attempts to chat her up, Sandy said 'you mean this is the first man whose attention you've paid any heed to Isabella, and there's a reason for that. It's because you like him,'

Letting that sink in for a few moments Isy finally nodded, a small, sharp, jerk of her head that was a simple acquiescence to both her friend and herself of a fact that she had desperately been trying to ignore for days.

'Well listen' responded Sandy gently becoming serious for a moment despite the titillation of the news 'you've done the right thing, taking a step back, it's easy to get swept up in theses things' she added, thinking back to when she first met her ex-husband and those heady days when she couldn't imagine her life without him.

'Spend the day with him tomorrow, don't think about anything else. Not the ramifications, what the kids might think or the world for that matter, given who he is. Just see if you're a match, see if you want to explore this further, and take it from there.'

Surprised at her friends' clarity of thought and sage advice, Isabella felt a weight lift off her shoulders. Sandy was right; it didn't have to be a "thing", not if she didn't want it to. She should just go with the flow, the universe had obviously put him in front of her for a reason; she just had to work out what that was.

The rest of the afternoon and the celebrations passed in something of a blur. She made all the right noises, well at least she hoped she did, although she did catch Ana staring at her strangely a few times and had to pull her mind back to attention into the present and try to follow the conversation around her. Finally it started coming to a natural end and she made her excuses and collected a by now very tired Luka and prepared to take her leave.

Laden with Tupperware filled to the brim with leftovers, she wouldn't have to cook for a week; she paused by her car to say goodnight to Sandy who was not looking forward to going to work.

'Thank you for coming' she remarked, knowing Ivan had a bit of a soft spot for her friend 'and thank you for your advice, it actually made me feel better, you know, calmer about things' she wiggled her eyebrows in Lukas direction indicating that the 'things' in question shouldn't be mentioned.

'Always here for you girl' Sandy replied, reaching in to give her friend a hug around the mountain of plastic in her arms 'just enjoy yourselves tomorrow' she added, including them both in the statement 'life's short you know' she added specifically to Isabella, who smiled at her to show she understood.

'Come on champ,' she called to her son, carefully pulling open the back door of the car and depositing her goodies on the seat 'let's get you home and bathed.' And with a final wave at Sandy she got them both into the car and made her way to the sanctuary of her house where she hoped she'd be able to get some sleep before their early start in the morning.

☼

Back in his basic, budget hotel room, he was keeping the rest of his expenses for a slap up meal and a drink or three, Derek was going through the photo's he'd taken today. He was thrilled for this unexpected turn up of a story, he'd expected to take some shots of Leonard looking morose by the pool or possibly getting sloshed in a bar while his sons looked sadly on if he was lucky. But this? This was pure gold and his senses were tingling in anticipation of the furore it was going to cause in the press.

With no qualms whatsoever he sent Angelica some shots of the type she requested, he'd caught a few of just Leonard and his boys coming out of the villa and a couple of nice ones of them on the horses and emailed her to say that he would get some more tomorrow on their scheduled trip to Hvar.

He then carefully selected a couple of teasing shots from the chain that captured the daring rescue and culminated in the picture perfect kiss and the group hug and sent them through to Dave at The Daily Rag, hugging himself with glee at what he knew would be the reaction. Knowing that it was late morning in Barbados he figured his colleague would just about be stirring from his current hangover and he should soon get a response.

Humming, he placed his phone on the nightstand and went to have a shower to get ready for tonight, he had booked a table at a highly rated restaurant up the mountain as a reward for today's efforts and was looking forward to spending Angelica's money in his favourite fashion immensely.

Roughly towelling his cropped hair dry as he came out of the bathroom he was unsurprised to see the phone flashing urgently at him and with a smirk, pointedly ignored it. He went to his suitcase and pulled out a pair of dark blue jeans and his favourite t-shirt, the colour of which, if his mother was to be believed, matched his blue eyes perfectly. Checking his image in the full length mirror on the back of the door he gave his reflection a wink of approval before finally sauntering over to the bed and picking up his phone.

There was a stream of increasingly urgent messages from Dave starting with "WTF???" and reaching DEFCON 1 by the last one, sent only moments ago which threatened to do unpleasant things to his manhood if he didn't respond immediately. Knowing he held all the cards firmly in his grasp, Derek calmly sent back a message, doubling the initial price of the job, and knowing that there would be some bluster before the inevitable acceptance of his price, happily put his phone on silent, slipped it into his back pocket and perched his Ray Bans on his head before heading out the door.

Sandy, who'd just had time to run some dry shampoo through her hair and slip on her favourite little black dress before donning her heels and going to the restaurant, looked up with interest when a lone man walked in shortly after she arrived.

'Table in the name of James' he stated without preamble when she sashayed across to welcome him. Looking at the diary on the lectern placed conveniently by the entrance, she turned her smile up a notch 'table for one?' she enquired and gestured that he follow her up to the terrace.

'Table for one but drinking for two' he responded as he followed her and took his seat at the table barely glancing at the view 'I'll have a scotch on the rocks to start and see where we go from there' he said, unashamedly roaming her body with his eyes.

'Right away Mr James' she replied, meeting his eyes without flinching, two could play at this game and he was extremely cute, it had been a while since her interest had been pricked by a man.

As the evening progressed she batted back his flirtations with practiced ease, making sure that he got an eyeful as she bent to serve plates at the few tables that came in that night and by the end of the evening was sitting at his table chatting easily as the waitress cleared the last tables, casting angry glances her boss for leaving her with all the work.

'So Derek, what brings you to our little island' she asked ignoring the waitress who pointedly stomped by angrily.

'I'm here for work' he replied, taking a sip of the red wine he had enjoyed with his meal then proffering the carafe to her inquiringly. Leaning over to the next table and grabbing a clean wine glass in response she held it up whilst he poured a healthy measure for her.

'And what kind of work brings you to Brač?' she asked before taking a grateful sip, amazed how her day had turned out. Most of the restaurant's clientele were very much attached holiday makers or local families so she didn't often get the chance to meet anyone single. And she was glad to find that Derek was as charming as he was good looking, she was thoroughly enjoying his company and gazing into his vivid blue eyes.

'I'm a photographer' he announced deliberately vaguely, having learnt long ago that revealing his actual job often lost him tit bits of information that helped him track down his prey or as in this case, opportunities to get to know gorgeous women like this one. Some people took umbrage at his profession for some reason, the irony that they were usually the same people that bought The Daily Rag and its ilk was not lost on him but the complexities of the general public's psyche was something he'd long ago given up trying to work out. Sandy, who just assumed he was either here to take photos of hotels and apartments for some holiday company or a travel blog or suchlike thought no more of it and happily acquiesced to his suggestion that they should continue their evening at a bar down in Bol.

Derek was delighted; he had not been expecting to meet a sassy, beautiful woman this evening, or any time soon for that matter. As much as he enjoyed his work it was a lonely profession, constantly on the road, never knowing where he'd be from one day to the next and usually only with other press people for company, didn't leave much room for romance on any level. He had had relationships in the past of course, but they always petered out when his love for his work took precedence over the woman in his life. So this unexpected flirtation was a welcome break in his lonely existence.

☼

As he said goodnight to his sons, reminding them they had an early start for their trip tomorrow, Leonard thankfully closed the door to their room, glad to finally have a moment to think. Making his way downstairs, he padded out to the starlit terrace and sat at the table gazing at nothing at all, replaying today's events in his mind. He remembered the shock of fear for her safety flashing through him briefly before kicking his horse into action with only the fleeting concern for his sons before he chased after the wayward horse. And then the kiss, that amazing, time stopping, exhilarating kiss that had been unlike anything he had experienced before, God knows where that had sprung from but it had felt so right, he couldn't stop thinking about it.

As he checked the time he remembered Angelica's earlier messages, and guiltily sent her some of the pictures he'd taken of the meal at the villa and a few of yesterday at the beach and hoped it would be enough to satisfy her and the company that was funding this trip.

Thinking that it probably wouldn't assuage her wrath he added a few more that the boys had taken on the boat trip, and after a moment's hesitation, even the one Alex had taken, catching him just as he fell into the sea. There, that should prove he was keeping his end of the bargain, and with that thought he took himself up to sleep in his bed for a welcome change. But despite his best intentions, sleep eluded him, and he just lay there, eyes open, willing the morning to come quickly so he could see her again.

FAMILY AFFAIR

As the sun rose, bright and true in the cloudless sky the next morning, it discovered Leonard already seated at the table on the terrace, guitar in hand, and several coffees into the day. After a few pointless hours of trying to sleep, he had given up and, driven by thoughts of Isabella, was now putting the finishing touches to his song.

He heard the alarm he had set going off in the house and laughed at its futility this morning, but went through to the kitchen where his phone was charging, to silence it before it disturbed the boys. There was another half hour before he had to wake them, and he planned to have breakfast ready for them when he did. His phone showed a message from his agent and, taking a deep breath, imagining the tirade, he opened it and was pleasantly surprised. 'Well done, great stuff. Sure SR will be thrilled.'

If he hadn't been so distracted with his anticipation for the day ahead, he would have put a little more thought into his initial flash of suspicion to this unusually pleasant text from Angelica, but as it was, he swept the thought aside and happily began to make French toast.

When the boys emerged, tousle-haired and sleepy-eyed a while later; they were delighted to find their dad awake and alert in the kitchen, and happily singing along to the music coming from the Bose speaker nestled on the whitewashed shelf with the cups.

'Morning boys!' he called chirpily, causing them to glance at each other and grin in embarrassment at this strange character that was greeting them today. Dad in the mornings normally meant eating your breakfast quietly until he had drunk enough coffee to face the day, but today not only was he smiling, he was serving up delicious smelling toast with cinnamon liberally sprinkled on it. Happily sitting down at the table to eat, they chattered freely about the upcoming day and, keen to be on their way, helped Leonard clear up when they'd finished and ran upstairs to get dressed.

The doorbell rang at 7.15 promptly and Leonard raced to the door before his sons could react, like a kid hearing the call of an ice-cream van. Flinging it open, he stood and stared at Isabella, not believing she was finally here.

'Hey,' she said softly, smiling shyly at him.

'Hey yourself,' he replied, still gazing at her until Luka, bored with the interaction, ran through the doorway to see Alex and Ben.

It didn't take long to get organised and all of them

squeezed into Karl to drive up to Milna, where they were due to catch the morning ferry. In the back seat, the boys entertained themselves with a raucous game of eye spy to pass the journey, leaving Isabella and Leonard to fill the silence that had fallen between them in the front.

'How was the party?' asked Leonard for something to say. 'It was Luka's grandfather's birthday, wasn't it?'

'Yes, it was his 70th, it was great. They're lovely people and they adore Luka, of course. We enjoy spending time with them.'

Although he was intrigued as to what had happened to Luka's father, Leonard didn't feel comfortable yet asking her about something so personal, so he steered the topic onto safer subjects and asked about the island they were going to visit instead. Before they knew it, she was directing him down to the busy harbour at Milna and they easily found somewhere to park.

Isabella went to collect the tickets and as she led them onto the ferry, she said 'it's only about a forty-minute crossing and we have the return tickets for today's last boat at 2 pm so that should be plenty of time to have a look around the town.' Feeling more assured in her role as a tour guide, she happily chatted to Leonard and the group fell into an easy camaraderie, so by the time they arrived in Hvar, it felt like the most natural thing in the world for them to be together.

☀

Back in her apartment in Bol, Sandy groaned and rolled over, eyes snapping open when her arm came in contact with unfamiliar warmth. Memories of last night came seeping back, and she smiled sleepily and murmured 'good morning, gorgeous,' to Derek, who was just stirring. Answering her with a lingering kiss, he paused to ask, 'any chance of a cuppa?'

She laughed as she pulled back the covers and slid out. She'd forgotten the British obsession with tea she'd been here so long. 'I'm sure I have some lurking in the back of the cupboard,' she replied and went to investigate. A few minutes later, head stuck in the cupboard, she heard him shout 'SHIT' from the bedroom. Running back into the room, she found him hastily pulling on last night's quickly abandoned jeans and rummaging through the pile of cushions on the chair for his socks.

'What's the panic?' she asked, disappointed that he was leaving so soon.

'Sorry, doll, I was supposed to be on a boat 5 minutes ago. Got a job in Hvar today,' he said as he fumbled to lace up his shoes. Flicking on her iPad on the bedside table, she quickly brought up the ferry times 'ok, the next one leaves at 9, you have time for your cuppa and to get there with a few minutes to spare, so calm your jets.'

Liking the fact that she was so practical and had not even shown a glimmer of clinginess usually associated with these mornings, he relaxed a little and walked over to kiss her again. Hearing the kettle click off, she pulled away and smiled.'We can continue that later if you have time,' she teased and went to make the tea.

'What's so exciting in Hvar?' she called back over her shoulder as she reached into the fridge for the milk.

'Oh, just something my client wants me to capture. I'm sure I'll get what he wants even if I'm late,' he responded, walking in and taking the mug from her gratefully. 'I really enjoyed last night,' he said earnestly.

'I bet you did!' she teased flippantly.

'I mean it, Sandy. I mean about meeting you, spending time with you… the other stuff, well, that was just the icing on the cake!'

'I enjoyed meeting you too,' she replied, drinking from the mug of coffee she'd made, 'but I'm not delusional. How many days are you here for? Two? Three?'

'I'd say probably three, or maybe four, depending on how the job goes,' he admitted slowly.

'Well then, let's not pretend this is anything that it's not, and just enjoy ourselves, eh?' she smiled to show that she meant it. The words reminded her of the advice she had given Isabella yesterday, and she wondered how her friend was getting on. 'That's funny; my friend is going to Hvar today as well, obviously the place to be today.'

When Derek left, with the promise of meeting her later after she finished work, Sandy propped herself up back in bed with a pile of cushion, wrapped the blankets around her supine form and luxuriated for a moment before picking her iPad back up to scroll through Facebook and see what had been happening in the world overnight. A few minutes later, the word 'SHIT' resounded around the room for the second time that morning. Hastily throwing the covers aside, she ran into the lounge to find her bag and her phone. She needed to get hold of Isy immediately and give her the heads up that her face was plastered all over the British press and Social Media, along with that of Leonard Lupine.

☼

Blissfully unaware that their bubble was about to not only burst but explode spectacularly, Isabella and Leonard were wandering along the picturesque promenade and into the quaint town of Hvar. The cobbled main square lined with faded ochre buildings with terracotta roofs was bustling this morning with locals and tourists alike. They aimed towards the Cathedral of St. Stephen, which stood centurion-like at the far end, watching over the activity with stark authority. As they made their way into the hushed atmosphere of the church, Isabella whispered facts about its heritage to the rest of the group, explaining that despite its typically Dalmatian structure, the interior had been decorated by Venetian artists. Leonard was blown away by the grandeur of the building, and spent a long time examining the paintings and icons captured by their beauty.

'This place is wonderful,' he whispered to Isy when

she came to stand next to him. She smiled at him and said 'I think so too, but I believe our boys need something else to capture their interest' and nodded to where the three of them were huddled by the entrance, obviously impatient to leave, their natural exuberance restrained by the unspoken understanding that this was not somewhere you ran around noisily. Smiling at the sight of their plight, he nodded, and they made their way over to them, side by side, almost but not quite touching, and led them back out into the square and the sunshine.

'Ok, boys,' announced Isabella, 'how does exploring a fortress sound to you?' she asked to a round of exuberant cheers that made her laugh out loud. Even Leonard seemed thrilled at the prospect, so she led them towards the steep, winding path that would take them up to the Fortica Španjola, standing proudly and majestically over the town it protected.

Arriving at the top twenty minutes later, slightly winded by the climb, they paused to look out at the stunning view across the town and out to the Adriatic Sea before paying the entrance fee to explore the interior. The reconstructed fort evoked its former grandeur with its tower and the battlements, traces of which could still be seen. The boys loved the canons, pointing out to the sea ready to defend against marauding pirates, and they raced madly around the prison in the lower level while Leonard and Isabella admired the collection of amphorae collected from the local seabed.

When they emerged back into the sunlight, Leonard took the opportunity for another photoshoot for Angelica, spurred by her earlier message, against the backdrop of undeniably stunning views. Isabella laughed at some of the silly poses he pulled and, deciding to capture these moments for herself, searched through her bag for her phone. With a sinking feeling, when no amount of upending the contents revealed what she already knew, she realised it wasn't there. Feeling vaguely naked without it, it was part of her job to be available 24/7; she reassured herself with the fact she was pretty certain she'd left it in the car, and she was actually with her guest. It wasn't like she would miss an important work call.

When the photo shoot was over, she steered them to the lovely little bar inside the fort walls as she was feeling the need for a cold coffee on this warm October day, and after ordering for everyone she and Leonard sat and chatted, whilst the boys continued to play happily amongst the buttresses.

'So tell me a little about your life, Leonard,' she said when a lull occurred in their talk. She was keen to get to know more about the man sitting next to her, he revealed so little of himself.

'I'm not sure where to start, really,' he mouthed deprecatingly 'it's not very exciting, despite what you may read in the press.'

'Well, you'll have to forgive me,' she laughed 'I am one of those rare people who pay no attention to the press, much less the British press. I have to be honest; I had no idea who you were until I Googled you!'

Feeling rather reassured by this comment, Leonard

began to open up. He told her about his struggle to become an actor, the thrill of finally getting a role he could sink his teeth into and Angelica's nefarious plan for him to live the part off-screen as well as on. 'So now I find myself rather stuck,' he admitted. Everyone believes that I am DI Fierce through and through when nothing could be further from the truth!'

With the short time she'd spent with him, she knew in her heart of hearts that this was true, the only time she'd seen him being horrible, with hindsight, had been brought on by stressful situations, he slipped into his personae when he didn't know what else to do. Smiling at him, she strove to let him know she understood but had to ask 'and Rennie?' for her peace of mind.

'That was initially another Angelica plan, but I would be lying if I didn't admit I was completely smitten with her at first,' he admitted. 'She was, is, everything I'm not. Bold, confident, a real go-getter, you know? So when she asked me to marry her, I just said yes, it seemed the most natural thing in the world at the time and of course, the press loved it.' He looked sadly across to where the boys were playing.

'But after the wedding, she surprised me with the honeymoon that she'd organised. Not dissimilar to the one she is having now. I'd imagined two weeks of nuptial bliss to ourselves, but she, along with Angelica, had organised a press junket, all expenses paid for them, so we spent the entire time surrounded by inebriated newshounds. It was horrible, and that's when the wool fell from my eyes and I promised myself I'd end it when we got back, but it was too late. She announced she was pregnant with Alex when we landed, to a hoard of waiting photographers and journalists. What could I do? I'm sure detective Fierce could have cold-bloodedly left her, but I certainly couldn't.'

He stopped, obviously lost in the memories of that moment, and Isabella was overwhelmed by the urge to take him in her arms and hold him close. But very aware they were in a public place, and not completely oblivious to the looks he had been attracting, managed to resist the temptation. Although it was nothing like her situation, Luka had been created through love, no agendas attached. She did know what it felt like to be trapped, in a place not of your choosing.

'But you eventually broke free,' she said. 'I can't imagine how things were for you, but I understand how you felt trapped,' she admitted softly, causing Leonard's amber eyes to snap back and focus on hers.

'You feel trapped?' he asked, surprised. Her life seemed idyllic to him. And another round of drinks later, wine this time as it seemed to suit their mood, she had shared the whole story with him, including parts she hadn't even told Sandy. The guilt she felt about wanting to leave and the small part of her that wished she had never stopped at Brač at the start of her epic tour, something she rarely admitted, even to herself.

Discreetly sat at a table at the far side of the bar behind them, Derek checked the time and realised that if he was going to make the last ferry back to Brač, he'd have to get a move on. He packed away his camera, fairly satisfied with the shots he'd taken today, although it hadn't been as near as good as yesterday; no wild horses or snogging, unfortunately. But he'd managed to capture the couple's close headed moments and adoring glances enough times to keep his audience happy. Looking forward to getting back to base and another night with Sandy, there was a spring in his step as he made his way back down the hill to the port.

Sandy was pulling her hair out. She had tried to call Isabella a zillion times, but with no luck; she had never known her friend not to have her phone clamped firmly to her hip, especially when she was working. Not knowing what else to do, she decided to drive to Milna to meet the last ferry coming back from Hvar and try and catch Isy there, and let her know what was going on, hopefully before she was swamped by the press. All thoughts of Derek and the amazing night they had spent together were pushed from her mind, as concern for her friend's well-being mounted, and she raced to the port to support her.

Without her phone, and being so deeply engrossed in Leonard as their conversation had meandered through their hopes and dreams with an awful lot of 'me too!' moments, Isabella had lost her sense of time. It was only when she heard the mournful parp of the departing ferry's horn that she realised that it was after 2 pm and they had just missed the last ferry home.

'Oh my God,' she squealed, panicking, her mind racing, trying to think of a way to get them home, or failing that, a way of rewinding the clock about an hour. Without her phone and all her precious contacts, she felt lost and incapable of forming a sensible plan.

Leonard, watching her panic, felt the urge to help 'we could just stay the night here?' he suggested hopefully. 'We could book a hotel,' he looked at her inquiringly.

'We can't do that,' she snapped. 'We need to get back.' She could only imagine what people would say if they knew they'd stayed over, little knowing that the world was already dissecting their relationship. It didn't bear thinking about.

Suddenly remembering the business card that the taxi driver had thrust in his hand when he left them at the ferry in Split, Leonard said 'hold on just a tick' and walked over to the wall where he could make a call in peace to his number one fan in Croatia. A few minutes later, he walked back looking cocky and smiling 'all sorted' he announced triumphantly.

'What do you mean all sorted?' she demanded, unable to think of a way he could have possibly fixed this mess.

'At four O'clock our very own boat will arrive and take us home,' he crowed proudly, revelling in the look of wonder and gratefulness that appeared on her face. 'That gives us time for a bite to eat in town before we leave. Come on,' and he called the boys and stood looking expectantly at her. He was enjoying this new role of being the man in charge. It was an unfamiliar sensation, but he could get used to it.

Isabella was not enjoying it quite so much. Well, she quite liked someone else looking after her for a change, but she was so used to making all the arrangements and being in charge, she felt a little uncomfortable with it. Realising she had no choice; she stood and joined them to walk back to town, demanding to know how he'd managed it as they went. He laughingly admitted to her his faux pas with the parking in Split and how he had met Jakov and she couldn't help but giggle. It was so Leonard. The whole fiasco had his name stamped on it.

They had a wonderful lunch in the town square, soaking up the sun while the boys enjoyed yet more freedom to run around and exploring the shops that were dotted about. Ben returned to the table holding his camera aloft 'Dad, Dad can I get these developed?' he asked hopefully 'there's a shop just there that does it; it won't take long' he insisted.'

Happily giving in to his son's desire, Leonard counted out the money, which Ben took solemnly in his small hand and marched off to the shop. 'Go with your brother, Alex, make sure he's ok.' Alex nodded and trotted off after Ben, closely followed by Luka who was completely in awe of the older boy and followed him everywhere.

'I'm glad they get on so well,' smiled Leonard, trailing off as he realised he was going to add 'it will make things easier,' as he remembered his promise to

Isy that there were to be no big discussions today. He wasn't sure yet what was going to happen between them, but he knew that he was not going to let this wonderful woman go, and he didn't want to frighten her off by talking about things before she was ready.

A text arrived to let him know that their boat was pulling into port so he stood, smiling gallantly 'your carriage awaits m'lady' and laughing at his manner and with relief, Isabella stood, picking her bag up from where it hung on her chair and walking along with him to the store to collect the boys.

☼

Back on Brač, standing on the harbour front jigging from foot to foot in impatience, Sandy waited for the boat to finally pull in and start to offload its passengers. Towards the end, when the last stragglers were making their way off, she saw a figure she recognised and her eyes lit up involuntarily as she saw Derek make his way down the gangplank. She'd completely forgotten he had been going to Hvar. It was only when he paused, to hoist his equipment bag further onto his shoulder, that the penny started to drop with a resounding clang, and without even thinking she stormed over, heels clicking angrily on the concrete, and slapped him resoundingly across the face.

Dropping his bag and holding his face in surprise, Derek looked at her, confused and hurt. It wasn't the first time in his life a woman had slapped him, but he usually knew why before it happened.

'What the hell?!' he said angrily, rubbing his cheek, which was glowing red from the impact and had a nice white imprint of her hand on it.

'You bastard' she shouted 'it was you wasn't it, taking those pictures of Isabella and plastering them all over the place?'

Leaping to the obvious conclusion, he asked, 'you mean the girl that was slobbering all over Leonard Lupine yesterday?'

'Yes, the girl that spent the day with him yesterday,' she responded defiantly, refusing to use the word slobbering and Isabella in the same sentence. 'Is that what last night was about? You wanted to get close to me to get information about her?' she demanded angrily, feeling distraught that her libido would dump poor Isy in this mess.

Narrowing his eyes, Derek looked at her. 'I promise you, Sandy, I had no idea you even knew her. Think about it, did I even mention her or him, ask any questions? Seriously, I came to the restaurant because it has good reviews and I left with you because, well because I like you' he finished off.

The wind taken out of her angry sails, Sandy stopped and thought about the evening before, and as she calmed down, she had to concede that although they had talked about a hundred different things, Isabella had not been one of them.

'But it was you, taking the pictures?' He nodded, refusing to look sheepish - it was his job for God's sake - and stood, hands-on hip, looking defiantly at her.

Not sure exactly how she felt about his job yet, well,

certainly not in relation to his current story, Sandy decided to focus on the issue at hand. 'So, did you see them in Hvar? I wanted to warn Isy what was happening. She's going to hate all this press attention. '

'When I left them, they were still up at the fortress over there, looking at each other all lovey-dovey and oblivious to the rest of the world. That's probably why they were not on the ferry.'

'Damn it, I wanted to warn her, but she's not answering her phone,' said Sandy thoughtfully, a small frown wrinkling up her nose delightfully. Casting around for a way to get back into her good graces, Derek spotted the bright green car that he recognised as Leonard's ride for the week.

'Why don't you leave a note on the windshield?' he asked, pointing over to the car. 'That way she'll get the message, even if something has happened to her phone?' Conceding that this was probably her only option at this point, she hastily scribbled a note on a scrap of paper from her bag and firmly wedged it under a wiper blade.

That done, she turned to Derek. 'I'm still not thrilled with you,' she stated sternly. 'But if you want to take me for a drink, we can talk about it,' she added with a sly smile.

When Leonard came to a halt on the dock and hailed the young man on the deck of the boat, Isabella couldn't believe her eyes. Their ride home was a beautiful Catamaran, the likes of which she had often admired from afar but never had the chance to go aboard.

'After you,' said Leonard, revelling in the awed look on her face, and the barely controlled frenzy of the boys as he gestured towards the passerelle.

'Shoes off, everyone; he called as the boys scrambled to be first on deck. Holding her sandals daintily in one hand, as she carefully made her way up the narrow gangway, she was helped onto the deck by a handsome young man who, when he spoke, was very obviously French.

'Welcome on board' he smiled charmingly, 'I am Val; I am your captain, here to carry you home.' He announced grandly. Isabella couldn't help but giggle at this and combined with her complete relief that they were on their way, plus the fact she was on an incredible yacht and had had several glasses of wine, her giggles became a little hysterical. Staring at his mum in amazement, Luka joined in. His boyish chortles were infectious, and soon they were all howling with laughter, unable to stop. The captain stood by, more than a little nonplussed at this reaction. Swooning, he was used to the laughter he was not.

'I will start the engine and when we are on our way, we will be serving champagne on the front deck,' he said a little stiffly and stalked off to the cabin in disgust.

'I'm sorry,' said Isabella, wiping the tears away, 'I don't know what came over me.' Se smiled at Leonard. 'Thank you for organising this', she added, meaning every word. She didn't know what she would have done if he hadn't come so unexpectedly to the rescue. It wasn't long until they were on their way and motoring gently back towards Brač. Leonard and Isy had made themselves comfortable on the front deck and the boys were inevitably annoying the captain as he tried to steer, although he seemed to be taking it in good humour.

Sipping at the chilled champagne, served by the slightly dumpy, sour-faced stewardess, Isabella let out a contented sigh. She could get used to this kind of life. Pulling up short, she realised that she was contemplating a life with Leonard; she took a moment to review her feelings. She was definitely becoming more at ease with the idea. Today had been wonderful and she realised that she was looking forward to more of the same. As if reading her thoughts, Leonard, sitting beside her on the sofa, leaned in and gave her a tentative, enquiring kiss. He'd been resisting the urge all day, and finally could bear it no more. When she didn't pull away, his lips explored further, and soon they were both absorbed in the moment.

'Hi Mum,' a small voice piped up, right next to her ear, 'I'm gonna drive the boat!' proclaimed Luka happily, blissfully unaware that he'd ruined a perfectly good kiss.

'That's great Luka, I think you'll be good at that,' she answered with a small shrug at Leonard that said "kids, what can you do?"

Laughing quietly between themselves, they finally began to talk properly, admitting what was happening between them and where they could go from here; hesitantly at first, but gaining momentum as they gained confidence in each other and began to trust the emotions that had been welling up in this past week. Finally, being able to admit to her feelings, however, didn't stop Isabella's guilt-ridden angst coming to the fore.

'I can't leave Brač,' Isabella stated, a little defensively, as they began to discuss the logistics. 'It's Luka's home, and his grandparents would be distraught if we moved away.'

Taking her face gently in his hands, her cheeks tingling at his touch, he said, 'I wouldn't ask you to move anywhere you didn't want to be. Who's to say I couldn't move here, eventually?'

'I'm thinking that's not very practical for your work and weekend visits from the boys,' she laughed sadly, amazed at his simple outlook on the situation.

'Listen, Isy, I have no idea how this is going to pan out, but I want us to give it a try. What I am feeling for you, in such a short space of time,' he whispered with a look of wonder on his face, 'there's no way I'm just going to let that go.'

Smiling in response, a small flicker of hope and elation bubbling in the pit of her stomach, she replied, 'do you think we can make this work?'

Answering her with another kiss, all thoughts of the pitfalls involved in this relationship fled, and she lost herself once again, as they motored slowly towards Brač.

☼

Sitting harbourside in Bol, Sandy had today's Daily Rag spread out on the bar table between them, furrowing her brow in amazement as she flicked through the pages. 'I can't believe there's this much coverage,' she said to him.

'If you think that's a lot, wait until tomorrow. I bet you anything you like that the planes coming in today are filled with journalists and photographers and it won't take long for them to figure out who your friend is and descend on her like the plague they are' happily denouncing himself along with his colleagues as he took a sip from his pint.

'Every paper in the UK is going to want a piece of this story; my shots are just the start.' He placed his beer down on the table, turning the mat it sat on thoughtfully and, surprised, he found himself saying 'If your friend Isabella doesn't call you soon, it might be worth going to her house to see if she's back.' He looked at her seriously, 'I really don't think she's going to know what's hit her, after the way you've described how she is, I don't like to think of how the next days are going to be for her. We should find her. Is there somewhere she could hide out until this blows over?'

'She could come and stay with me,' Sandy responded, before looking at him suspiciously. 'You're not just saying this so you will know where she is?' Without meeting her eyes, he said remorsefully, 'Nah. I'm not known for my gallant gestures, but, well, she's your mate. And it sounds like the poor girl has been through enough shit already. I'll send that agent some of the shots of Leonard from today, but leave her out of it and withdraw from the circus event this is going to turn into.'

She stood up and walked around the small table to kiss him. 'Thank you, Derek, that means a lot to me.'

'Don't get all soppy,' he muttered, but she could see he was starting to blush, 'I've already made a wedge of cash from the first lot of pictures and it's good to have the reputation for finding a good story rather than jumping on the tail of one' he blustered and hid his face back in his drink.

Looking at the time, Sandy stated decisively, 'right, let's have another and if she doesn't call, we'll go and stake out her place until she arrives.'

'What about the restaurant?' he asked. 'Don't you have to open up in a bit?'

Tapping away at her phone as she messaged her ex, she said, 'don't worry about that, they can survive without me for one night. It's one of the many joys of being the boss!' Admiring her attitude, Derek sank the last of his beer and waved at the barman to bring another round.

They were all sorry when the boat slipped easily into the harbour at Milna and they had to say goodbye to their captain and the grumpy stewardess. As they disembarked, they felt briefly unbalanced by the solid ground and stood for a moment to find their land-legs. Leonard took the captain to one side and Isy saw money exchange hands but decided to ignore it, it wasn't as if she could afford to contribute anyway and she was sure Leonard would dismiss any such idea.

Returning to the car and pulling the scrap of paper from under the windscreen wiper, Leonard was relieved to see it wasn't a parking ticket and having read it, handed it to Isabella 'seems like your friend has been trying to get hold of you' he said as she read it. Slightly concerned that it might be something urgent, she searched around inside the car until she found her phone under the passenger seat, where it had slipped unnoticed from her bag.

Seeing it was out of battery, she said, 'oh well, I'll just have to call her when I get back. It's probably just another Sandy drama,' and smiled at Leonard as they started to drive back towards the villa. Once they had arrived, she took her leave, dragging herself away despite Leonard's protestations.

'I have to get home,' she laughed as he pleaded with her to stay a little longer, 'I have things to do at home and besides, we've already agreed that Luka and I will spend the afternoon with you all tomorrow.'

Begrudgingly, and with a last lingering kiss, he let her go, desperate for tomorrow to come but very aware it was the last official day of the holiday and he would have to leave. Shaking his head to dislodge that thought, he walked back into the villa where the boys had flopped onto the sofa and turned on the TV, too tired to demand some more pool time. As they flicked through the channels to find Cartoon Network, Alex stopped mid-channel hop and called to his dad who had gone into the kitchen, 'hey Dad, there's a picture of us on the telly!'

Wandering back through, munching on a biscuit, Leonard nearly choked when he saw the images on the screen. He didn't need to speak Croatian to get the gist of what the newscaster was happily saying and put his hand on the back of the sofa to steady himself.

'I'm going to bloody kill Angelica!' he exclaimed before stamping off angrily to get his phone.

☼

Isabella had just put her phone on to charge and was happily pottering around the kitchen when she heard an urgent knocking at the door. Dancing over to it, she called, 'hold your horses,' and opened it to find a worried-looking Sandy with an extremely attractive man standing on her doorstep.

'What's the matter?' asked Isy, coming rapidly down from her high. 'Is it Anna? Ivan?' she asked, suddenly panicking that something had happened to them and she had been drifting around in her love-struck haze whilst they needed her.

'No, no, it's nothing like that,' said Sandy reassuringly, as she walked in. 'It's this,' and she held up a newspaper in front of Isy's face. Pushing it back a little so she could make out what was written there, the colour drained from her face as she read the bold headline, "Lupine's Revenge," and took in the photograph underneath. Which was a crisp, clear shot of her and Leonard, clinched in a scorching kiss, with the sea innocently acting as a perfect, romantic backdrop.

'Come and sit down,' said Sandy, taking her ashen friend by the arm and leading her to the sofa. Nodding her head at the bottles on the sideboard, she motioned for Derek to do the honours. Trembling now, Isabella sat and started to read through the story which ran several pages through the paper.

Despite being told that our favourite detective was off licking his wounds as his ex-wife enjoys her honeymoon, we can exclusively reveal that he is far from heartbroken. In fact, he is sweeping this secret, sexy girl off her feet, quite literally, after a daring horseback rescue when her mount went mad on the small island of Brač in Croatia. Obviously wanting to show Rennie that he is getting along quite nicely without her, he's made a big show of his new amour and spent the day with her yesterday.

Throwing the paper to one side, unable to read any-more, she gratefully took the glass being offered to her by the stranger. Unaware of what it was and not car-ing, she downed it in one as her anger started to rise. "That bastard," she thought "after all that, all those sweet nothings and it meant nothing, just another publicity stunt to keep him in the headlines."

She was furious, almost speechless with anger, but managed to find the strength to say 'I think I'd like you to leave now' to Sandy and then looking over at the man 'I'm sorry, I have no idea who you are, but I need to be alone right now.'

Sandy was shocked. She'd never seen Isabella look

so fierce, and deciding it was best to let her calm down, started to back away towards the door, pulling Derek with her. 'I'll call you in a bit,' she called to a blank-faced Isy, who remained seated on the sofa, not even glancing up.

'Let me know if you need anything,' she added, hoping for a response. Seeing that there wasn't going to be one, she took Derek with her outside and gently closed the door and leaned against it. 'My God, she looked angry,' she whispered. Not truly understanding where Isabella's anger was coming from didn't lessen her shock at her friends' reaction.

Derek nodded in agreement.'You did the right thing, but we should let her know that she needs to get out of here.' They stood staring at each other for a moment, not sure what to do.

'I vote we give it half an hour and then try again,' said Sandy finally. 'Let's just wait in the car for a bit,' and they walked back over to his jeep to wait.

Inside the house, Isabella was shaking. She wasn't sure if it was shock, anger or heartbreak, but she was not feeling well. Luka, who had been playing happily in the garden while her world imploded, came running in.

'I'm hungry, Mum,' the small boy announced, planting himself firmly in front of her in a way that she recognised that meant he wouldn't move until she obliged. Thankful for something normal and mundane to do, she forced a smile and answered, 'come on then, Champ' and led the way into the kitchen to prepare something for him. There was no way she could stomach anything right now.

It was only when he was firmly ensconced on the sofa, eating some reheated leftovers from his grandfather's party, and watching his favourite show that she finally turned her phone on. It instantly sprang to life with a constant stream of messages, missed calls from Sandy all day and, more recently, from Leonard, along with a lengthy message. Not even bothering to read what it said. After all, what could he say that would make this OK? She started tapping out her angry response. She made it very clear what she thought of him and his low life, double-dealing tactics and even more clear that she never wanted to see him or hear from him again and used some expletives that Sandy would be very surprised that she knew, to emphasise exactly how she felt.

Taking a deep breath, she sent it, and forcing herself not to cry, deleted his messages and then all his details from her contacts, emptying her email trash for good measure. That done, she went to take a shower, hoping to wash her feelings of degradation away under the hot jets of water in her small bathroom.

LONDON CALLING

Leonard was on the phone with Angelica when Isabella's text came through and didn't notice it immediately. He had spent ages trying to track down his agent before finally reaching her and was engrossed in her fairy-tale of innocence with regards to the blow-up of publicity in the press.

'I wish I could lay claim to it, dear, its pure genius!' She drawled convincingly. 'All that macho galloping to rescue a damsel in distress was absolute gold. You have no one to blame but yourself you know, if you'd had the nice quiet holiday that we'd planned, none of this would have happened.'

Conceding that she had a point, and completely forgetting to ask about how a photographer had found him in the first place, he glanced at the message that had come through, his face lighting up when he saw her name then dropping in disbelief when he read the raging missive.

Heart sinking beyond his flip-flops, he stood for a

moment, stunned. How could she dismiss him so easily? He could understand her horror at being photographed and plastered all over social media. It wasn't everyone's cup of tea, but to just throw what they had out the window with a text? His insecurities came steaming to the fore, and he found solace in their familiarity. Maybe she hadn't felt the same as him after all; maybe all that talk of trying to make their relationship work was just that, idle talk, and she wasn't prepared to look beyond this, their first hurdle. That must be it. Stupid to think otherwise, really. Just like Rennie, she had used him for whatever purpose, probably to make sure he gave the blasted holiday company good feedback.

Hardening his heart and calling on DI Fierce for support, he snapped 'Angelica, I want to come back to London. We both know I'm not going to get any peace, now the press has got hold of this. Book me on a flight as soon as you can!'

Relieved that he wasn't investigating the whole photographer debacle any further, she quickly tapped away at her MacBook and pulled up a list of the next flights leaving from Split back to London. 'There's an EasyJet tonight at 10 pm. Do you think you can make it?'

'I'll make it, even if I have to bloody walk,' he snapped stupidly.

'Well, unless you can walk on water, I'd better check the ferry schedule', she replied tongue in cheek, not wishing to push any more of his buttons. 'OK, if you get the 7.30 ferry you will have just enough time.'

He could hear her fingers tapping madly away on the keyboard down the line. The only hitch is the car hire company office at the airport won't be open. You'll have to leave the car at the port office and get a taxi.'

Knowing exactly who he was going to call, he responded, 'that's fine, send through the boarding passes' and ended the call abruptly. Turning to where his sons were still watching TV, 'Boys, get your stuff together, we have to leave' he called to the startled faces looking up at him from the sofa.

'But why Dad' whined Alex, 'we were supposed to have another day, and Isabella is coming tomorrow with Luka' he insisted. At the sound of her name, his insides curled up. 'For once in your life, can you do as I tell you, and just get your stuff together, and quickly, we have a ferry to catch,' he shouted. Shocked at his reaction, both boys got up meekly and plodded upstairs to do as they were told. He could hear Ben sniffling, trying not to cry. Leonard felt dreadful, but he knew he had to keep moving forward. The sooner he left, the sooner he could leave this situation behind and get on with his sad, lonely life.

Steeling himself, he called Jakov, who was delighted to hear that his favourite TV star would need his assistance again so soon, and readily agreed to meet him off the ferry a little later that night. It was a subdued group that finally left the villa a short while later. Leonard nearly cracked when Ben proffered one of his precious photographs. 'Can I leave this for Isy?' he asked meekly. 'I want her to have something to remember us by.'

He looked at it; it was the shot Sandy had taken of them all at the beach bar. A picture that showed a happy family group smiling at the photographer, his heart splintered at the image, and poking it into one of the Sublime Retreats envelopes provided, he scrawled 'For Isy' quickly on the front and left it on the table by the front door.

Just before he pulled the door shut for the last time, he stopped suddenly, and searching through his bag to find it, pulled out the paper that had the last draft of his song on it. He tucked it sadly into the envelope next to the photo. He knew he would never sing this song; it would be too painful to even think about, so there was no point keeping it, and with that mournful thought, he firmly shut the door.

Having allowed herself a good cry in the shower, Isabella felt a trifle better, but rubbing her hair dry as she looked in the mirror, she could see she looked dreadful. Puffy-eyed and lacklustre was the best description she could think of. Walking through to her bedroom, she planned on putting on her comfies and binge eating whatever was left in the fridge. She was surprised when she went back downstairs, brushing her hair as she went, to find Sandy and her mysterious stranger had returned and Luka was happily chatting with them as he finished eating his dinner.

All three looked up as she came down the stairs. Luka with his usual sunny smile and the adults with measured concern on their faces.

'Hi, how are you doing?' asked Sandy, getting up from the armchair to go over to her friend and enveloping her in a hug. Isabella stood, unresisting for a moment, appreciating her friend's gesture, before pulling away and putting on her bravest face.

'I'll survive,' she said sourly, and tried to temper it with a smile. 'So, who's this?' she nodded over at the man sitting next to her son.

'Ah, this is Derek. We met yesterday.'

'I'm not sure that this is the best time for meeting your latest fling Sandy, I do have other things on my mind' murmured Isabella, trying to say it quietly, not wanting to be rude even now.

Derek, who couldn't help but overhear her, stood up and walked towards her. 'I'm afraid I may be the cause of those things,' he said and when she looked confused added 'those things on your mind, I guess you mean the photos?'

Nodding at the stranger, not sure where he was going with this, she looked at him expectantly, waiting for him to continue. He stood unspeaking for a minute, seeming unable to form the words, but after an urgent, encouraging nod from Sandy, 'I'm the photographer, I took those pictures of you and Leonard,' he blurted out. Her reaction was feral. Without thought, she launched her hairbrush, the only missile she had to hand, straight at him and caught him squarely above his left eye.

He shouted 'fuck' loudly and his hand flew to his face, clasping the wound but unable to staunch the flow of blood that was spurting out of it.

'Oh my God, oh my God, I'm so sorry' Isabella cried, running to the kitchen to grab some paper towels to staunch the flow and swiping his hand away to apply it firmly. Sandy, who'd been standing by in shock throughout this drama, was glad to see that the nice Isabella was still in there, despite the beating she had taken today.

As Isabella lifted the already soaked paper to check the damage and gently dabbed at the cut Sandy said 'I think introductions are in order, Isabella this is Derek, the ratbag photographer, and Derek, this is my best friend Isabella whose life you have just ruined.'

Smiling awkwardly at Derek before turning to Sandy, 'I'm pretty sure all this is not his fault,' she responded and turned back to a startled looking Derek.

'I'm pretty sure it is' he demurred, 'I'm the one who took the pictures that are now splashed all over the media,' he added, just to make sure she understood the situation.

'I get that,' she answered, pulling away the now sodden paper and walking back to the kitchen to throw it in the bin and get the first aid box out from the cupboard. 'But you were only doing your job' she called back to him, as she rooted through the box for a Band-Aid. 'If that horrible man hadn't set me up, you wouldn't have been there,' she added firmly, stripping the wrapping from the plaster before expertly applying it to his eyebrow.

It took a moment before the other two got it; they glanced at each other, understanding Isy's reaction so much better now. 'Isabella,' began Sandy, walking over to look her in the face 'it wasn't Leonard that set this up, it was his agent.'

What little colour there was left, drained from her face as Isabella queried, 'but he knew, he was in on it?' stumbling over the words in haste, as if that would somehow make them true.

Derek shook his head emphatically. 'Uh-uh, he didn't know anything about it. There's no way he would be involved in something like this. He hates the press and works very hard at keeping his personal life out of the limelight.'

Sinking onto the nearest chair, Isabella's head was whirling. This put a completely different spin on things. She still hated the fact that her face was splashed all over the place, but if he didn't organise it, he was probably equally furious. They'd even discussed how they were going to handle the first stories about them when the press eventually cottoned on, and telling him to bugger off had not been part of the plan.

Grabbing her phone, she desperately checked to see if he had contacted her again, but there was nothing. She frantically checked through all her apps to see if there was any trace of him left, but she'd done a top-notch job of deleting him from her life.

Looking up desperately, 'I have to go to the villa' she insisted, looking from one face to the other. 'I need to tell him that it's OK, that I didn't mean what I said.'

'I don't think that's a good idea,' Derek replied gently, hunkering down in front of the stricken looking woman. 'My guess is, a planeload of reporters will be here by now, probably camped outside the villa. That's why we came back, to warn you that you should leave for a couple of days until this blows over.'

Seeing Isabella's look of panic, Sandy quickly interjected, 'it's ok hun, you and Luka can come and camp out with me. It'll be fun' she added, as she noticed the small boy was now paying attention to the conversation and had a worried air about him.

'That's wonderful, thank you,' Isy smiled, 'but I still have to go and see Leonard tonight. I must let him know... well, you know.'

'That you love him?' Sandy smiled, thrilled to see that her friend had finally found someone worth fighting for. Isabella nodded, a look of wonder on her face, as the enormity of what she had just admitted sank in. She stood up decisively. 'Right, Sandy, you throw together a bag of stuff for me and him,' she nodded over at Luka, 'and go to your place. And you,' she looked at Derek, 'can take me to the villa. If necessary, you can distract your fellow cohorts while I sneak around the back.'

'I'll have to take your car,' Sandy called as she headed up the stairs. 'No problem' shouted Isabella, 'keys are in it.' Feeling much better now that she had a plan, Isabella went and sat next to a perplexed Luka on the sofa.

'Luka, we are going to have a sleepover with Auntie Sandy, won't that be fun?' she asked, trying to inject excitement into her voice. Luka, who loved staying at Sandy's place at the best of times - she always let him eat sweets - was quite happy with this new arrangement and nodded enthusiastically. 'OK, run upstairs and help her grab a few things and then she'll take you to her flat. Mummy has something to do first.'

As Luka happily trotted off she laughed, 'Oh to be a kid again, nothing fazes them'. She turned to Derek, 'right, come on you. Let's go and try and salvage this relationship.'

☼

As the ferry approached Split, Leonard sat morosely on the upper deck as Alex and Ben ran around, hyper from a sugar rush; he'd unprotestingly bought them Gummy Bears and a Coke as they boarded. Guilt at cutting their holiday short and shouting at them earlier combined with the general feeling of melancholy that had settled over him like a cloak, had led to him not thinking through his response, and he was now paying the price.

'Look, Dad, I can see the harbour!' shouted Ben, leaning forward on the railings precariously, jigging up and down in his high. Alarmed Leonard called 'come away from there, boys' urgently and they obliged and started to run up and down the gangway again.

Thankfully the boat wasn't busy so they weren't really annoying anyone, except for a little old lady near the doors, who sat hunched with her small dog on her lap, who continually growled and yapped at their passing, causing her to scowl every time they belted past.

Uncaring, Leonard stood and walked up front to watch the boat arriving on the mainland and it wasn't long before he could make out the maniacally waving Jakov on the jetty, standing in front of his gleaming taxi. With a brief wave to the driver, Leonard turned and called the boys to heel before going down to the parking level and the car. The unloading process was interminable, seeming to take forever, but eventually, the lorry in front of him released its breaks and with a loud hiss and a puff of putrid fumes from the exhaust, started to drive down the ramp.

Pulling up alongside Jakov, he opened the window and smiled. Seeing a familiar face made the situation seem more bearable somehow.

'Jakov, my friend, how are you?'

'Very happy, Mr Lupine! Very happy to see you again but sad that you are leaving so soon. Did you not like it here?'

Quick to reassure him, he said, 'we absolutely loved it here; I just have work things...' he petered out, hoping that Jakov would take him at his word. Seemingly satisfied, the man looked across to where a row of single-storey, prefabricated offices stood and pointed over with a meaty arm.

'That's where you need to go for the car,' he told Leonard 'I checked for you, they are waiting.'

Closing the window, Leonard put the car into gear and drove slowly across to the parking area on one side of the buildings, the flags of the different hire companies dancing gaily in the light breeze that had sprung up, adding a chill to the air.

Pulling the suitcases from the boot, as the boys clambered noisily out of the back, Leonard felt like he was sleepwalking, so surreal did the situation feel. Just a few hours ago, he was kissing the woman he thought loved him the way he loved her. Planning their future together and looking forward to what that might bring. Now here he was, standing in the industrial landscape of a ferry port, heading back to where he didn't want to be, with two hyper children in tow. Surely this was a bad dream? Every step forward felt more and more like the wrong decision, but he didn't know what else to do. Telling his sons to get into the taxi and wait for him, he took the keys for Karl into the office, and after a quick inspection, he was told he was free to go.

Sliding into the front seat, he nodded to Jakov, and the taxi took off with its usual gusto and dived into the throng of traffic on the main road before Leonard had time to put his belt on.

'There may be a small delay with your flight,' mentioned Jakov conversationally as he zipped in between the lanes of the road leading to the airport. 'I have an app, I check these things,' he added proudly 'and I think there has been some troubles, some, how do you say, striking?'

'You mean strikes?' asked Leonard, glad to talk about something else. 'The airport staff are striking?'

Jakov, nodding violently, said 'Yes! That's it, the staffs are striking. But not here,' he added in case Leonard thought the Croatians were to blame for the delay. 'In France, bloody bastards,' he muttered. 'Made delays all day.' He harrumphed to emphasise his disgust with the nation. Arriving at the airport in record time, Jakov insisted on stopping in the long-term car park and taking them into the terminal. He wasn't going to let his favourite star go until the last minute.

Leonard was thankful that he did. As the driver took the suitcases, it left him free to marshal the boys, who were showing no signs of slowing down. Inside the terminal, it was chaos, crowds of travellers crammed into the small space, their tired demeanours and lounging positions confirming the report of delays, and Leonard's heart sank for the second time that day. At Jakov's insistence, he stood with the bags and the boys, while the burly driver forced his way through to the check-in desk to find out what was going on.

He returned quickly, 'as I said, is a little late.'

'How late is a little late?' asked Leonard frustrated; he now just wanted to get moving and get this journey over and done with.

'Ah, I think one, maybe two hours. Not so much' was the casual reply, leaving Leonard spluttering in annoyance.

'Let us get you checked in, give the bags, then we go to the bar up there.' Jakov pointed to the upper level. 'I waits with you, no problem for that,' and happily grabbed the bag handles before Leonard could react. When they made it to the front of the check-in queue and were bag free, they all squeezed into the glass lift that took them to the next level. Striding forward, Jakov led the way, being greeted as they entered the small café by the waiter, who exclaimed loudly and hugged him vigorously and, after much delighted chatter, was brought over to meet Leonard.

'This is my brother Michael,' announced Jakov happily, slapping the younger man on the back so hard he staggered forward into Leonard's proffered hand.

'Happy to meet you, Michael,' Leonard responded, eyes now greedily roving the shelves behind the bar to see what was on offer.

They found a table and placed their order. He firmly refused to let the boys have any more coke, so they opted for juice instead, and Leonard and Jakov selected a draft beer.

'So, how many brothers do you have?' asked Leonard conversationally as they waited for the drinks to arrive. He was salivating, watching as Michael pulled the pint.

'I am one of six,' he replied. 'I am the eldest and Michael is the youngest,' he said loudly as the waiter approached. It was obviously a source of amusement. Being an only child, Leonard couldn't imagine what it was like to have that kind of relationship, but he could see that they loved each other very much. "I hope Alex and Ben feel the same when they grow up," he thought, looking at the boys fondly as they sat, heads together, absorbed in a game on the iPad. He was pleased to note it was the first time they'd turned it on since the holiday began, which made him happy. He must have been doing something right in that department, at least.

Checking his phone for the millionth time to see if Isy had changed her mind and messaged, he saw that there was nothing, and his face fell. He picked up his glass 'here's to a life without women,' he announced passionately before downing half the glass in one easy to swallow.

Looking at him speculatively, Jakov said, 'Ah, so that's how it is, my friend. I wondered. This morning you ask me to arrange a boat ride for you and your lady friend and then here you are a few hours later looking shit and heading home. What happened?'

Glancing at the boys but seeing they were paying absolutely no attention to the adults at all, Leonard started to tell his tale. Once he started, he found he couldn't stop, and he poured his heart out to the older man. Not leaving anything out, he described his miserable life in London, his horrible ex-wife, his desire to be a singer and finally, Isabella.

He told Jakov how she lit up the room, how she used a pen to hold her mass of curls in a bun, how she could cook like an angel and had been more of a mother to his boys these last few days than their real mum had been in months. And then he told of the press invasion of their bubble, popping it with a pin so sharp it couldn't be ignored, and she had told him she didn't want him in her life. Jakov listened patiently, not interrupting and nodding in all the right places.

It was only when Leonard finally stopped that he looked at him inquiringly and asked, 'so what in the damn hell are you doing here? Running away like a coward, you say she has given up at the first hurdle, but it sounds to me like you have.'

Shaking his head sadly, Leonard replied, 'she made it pretty clear that she didn't want to see me again, Jakov, and I don't blame her.' His voice was truculent now with heartbreak. 'Who would want to be part of my miserable life?'

Before he could respond, the screens overhead suddenly sprang to life with a clicking sound and everybody looked up to see that a fleet of flights had landed and boarding gates had been assigned. Standing up decisively, Leonard said quickly, 'looks like this is us, come on boys,' hoping if he kept moving forward it would make this easier. Tutting loudly his disapproval, Jakov eased his large frame from the chair with a groan and asked 'if that is your decision?'

'Yup,' Leonard replied, trying to sound nonchalant, and pulled his phone out to bring up their boarding passes, ready for the attendants at the gate. Standing before security, Jakov enveloped him in a bear hug that left him breathless, but smiling.

'Sretan put. Travel well my friend and remember, if you ever come back, Jakov is always at your service!'

Nodding bravely, trying to hide the tears that were threatening, Leonard shooed the boys towards the line for the bag scanners and pulled up a tray to load their things onto. Only when they had successfully passed through and were collecting their belongings on the other side did he look back. Jakov was still standing there, watching him protectively, a misty-eyed look on his face. With a last smile and a wave, Leonard turned and walked towards gate number four, leaving small pieces of his happiness, like a trail of breadcrumbs behind him.

☼

Pulling up outside the villa, Isabella glanced around to check, but there was no sign of any press or photographers.

'Looks like we've beaten them to it,' grinned Derek happily, relieved not to have to deal with them on her behalf.

'It also looks like he's not here' said Isabella, who could see there was no car in the drive and no lights on inside. She thought for a moment before saying, 'I'll just go in and leave him a note. I think that's the best I can do right now.' She opened the car door and slung her bag over her shoulder, walking quickly up to the front door, her sense of urgency driven as much by her desire to communicate with Leonard as by her fear of a hoard of press hounds descending any minute now. She rooted through her bag until she found the keys and swiftly let herself in.

She knew instantly that something was wrong. She had been in this house enough times to know how it felt when it was empty. She stood for a moment in the dark hallway, senses alert, straining to feel something, anything that would prove what her heart already knew, to be wrong. Moving slowly into the lounge, she flicked on a light and looked around. Room by room, she did the same, but found nothing.

All traces of Leonard and his boys were gone. It was

only as she came back down the stairs, turning off the lights as she went, that the enormity of what this meant hit her. He had fled, run away without a backwards glance because of that one message. Her heart, which had been torn earlier by the thought that he'd used her, now completely cracked and she slid down the wall in the hallway sobbing, unable to go any further.

That's where Derek found her a short while later, when he went to investigate what was taking so long. Trying to push the front door open, he found it obstructed, and peering around the gap and looking down, he saw her there, curled up in a foetal position, tears, silently now, running down her face. With a deep sigh, he gently pushed the door a little further so he could squeeze in, and without saying a word, lowered himself to the ground and took her in his arms.

In the time it took for her to stop the tears, he had taken in the empty-looking lounge and put two and two together. He angled his body so he could pull the travel pack of tissues from the pocket of his jeans, and struggled to pull one out with his arm trapped behind her, gently leaned her back against the wall.

'He's gone, huh? He asked, passing her the now freed tissue. Wiping her eyes before bending her head to facilitate blowing her nose, she included a small nod in the motion.

'Well, he probably wanted to get out before the circus begins' said Derek sagely, 'he's hugely protective of his boys, he doesn't like them exposed to the limelight.'

'That may be true, but the fact that he's left without saying anything means he doesn't care anymore,' she sniffed, trying not to start crying again. 'He must hate me now, all those horrible things I wrote in that message. I can't believe I was so heartless,' she added, hiccupping back another sob.

'Well, we can't do anything about that sitting in this dark hallway' Derek smiled, trying to lighten the mood. 'Let's get you to Sandy's place where I'm sure we can come up with some kind of plan to sort this mess out.' And he stood, pulling her gratefully to her feet, and led her back out to the car. Neither of them noticed the small envelope propped on the table.

☼

When the plane landed at Gatwick, Leonard was relieved to see no sign of the press as they walked out of the baggage claim hall, just a discreet sign saying "Leonard" held by the driver that Angelica had sent to meet them. His sons quickly fell asleep in the cocoon of warmth in the car and left him free to gaze out of the window, watching the early morning London streets slide by. He felt numb. The last 24 hours had been an emotional rollercoaster and had left him unable to feel anything. Even the sight of a pair of urban foxes, which usually brightened his mood, was unable to elicit a reaction from his exhausted soul.

Back at his flat, he got the boys into their pyjamas and settled into his bed for the few hours left of the night. Walking back into the lounge, he briefly debated whether to pull out the sofa bed, but knowing he wasn't going to get any sleep tonight, decided against it and settled for pulling out a bottle of whiskey instead.

A subdued Isabella and Derek arrived back at Sandy's apartment, Derek discreetly taking Sandy to one side to let her know what had happened at the villa, and Isabella, zombie-like, joining Luka on the sofa. She sat staring at nothing while the small boy chattered on. If she had known that her demeanour directly reflected that of Leonard's, all those miles away, it might have brought her small comfort. But as it was, she believed he didn't care and had happily headed back to his hedonistic lifestyle in London without looking back.

Once Luka had been persuaded to go to sleep in the spare room, the three of them went out onto the balcony, which afforded a wonderful view over the bay. As she sat gazing at the lights, Isabella remained introspective until she was startled from her reverie by Sandy plonking a glass of wine down noisily on the table in front of her.

'Snap out of it girl and get some of that down you' she insisted, taking the seat opposite 'brooding doesn't suit you.' And she gestured to Derek to join them.

'I'm not sure what else I can do' said Isabella sadly. 'Or rather, I'm not sure there's any point doing anything.'

'I thought you wanted to get a message to him?' asked Derek.

'I did. But now I don't see the point. He obviously didn't care enough to stay, even if I was horrible in my message. You would think if he had feelings for me he would have tried again, don't you, tried to explain that it was nothing to do with him?' she asked the couple, looking to justify her feelings.

'I'm not so sure,' observed Derek, who had had some experience with the man, albeit from behind a camera. 'I can honestly say that the shots I took of the two of you in Hvar were pictures of a couple in love. I've seen enough of the other kind to know the difference. He would have been pretty cut up by what you wrote'

'Maybe we can get a message to him?' speculated Sandy hopefully, still wanting her friend's love story to have a happy ending.

'I could get a message to him through Angelica, his agent,' said Derek, leaning forward, folded arms resting on the table as he looked seriously at Isabella. 'She owes me a favour or two.'

Even though her heart leapt at the idea, Isabella shook her head. She couldn't face more rejection and heartache. If they sent a message and he didn't respond, she would be wounded beyond repair.

'Isabella.' began Sandy sternly 'stop this nonsense. I have never known you to run away from anything and certainly not something as important as your happiness.' She stood and poured more wine into the three glasses. 'Let Derek get a message to him and let's sort this out. You're both dotty about each other and I refuse to see that go down the pan because you're too scared to let your feelings be known.'

The smile on her face when she finally looked up at Sandy told the other two all they needed to know about her decision. She was illuminated with hope, her eyes shining and the whisper of a smile returning to her lips.

'What could I say' she murmured, almost to herself, her mind now racing with possibilities as she looked down at her hands on her lap, turning them over and rubbing at the right with the thumb of the left as if reviving the love line there.

'You could start with the truth,' Sandy asserted blandly, smiling at her friend's concerned features. 'You've always been good at that,' she laughed. 'Have a think about it tonight and you can write in the morning with a clear head. He will have barely got home about now, I would imagine, so a few more hours won't hurt!'

☼

When Leonard finally surfaced from his drunken snooze the next day, he was glad to see that the boys were still sound asleep. Their night-time travelling had done them in and they were both still curled up in bed, exactly as he had left them a few hours before. Smiling at them for a moment before gently shutting the door to the bedroom, he padded back into the kitchen to down some aspirin and make some coffee.

While the machine worked its magic, he switched on his phone, hoping deep down that a message from

Isy would be the first thing he'd see. But his hopes were resoundingly squashed, as the first message was from Angelica and of Isabella there was no sign. Sitting sadly down on the stool by the breakfast bar, he took his first sip of the restorative nectar and opened the demand for communication from his agent. Seeing that she wanted to speak to him, he decided to get it out the way and called her immediately.

'Good morning, Leo,' she answered brightly on the first ring, causing him to scowl down the phone. 'I take you got back OK?'

'Yes, everything went smoothly. Thank you.'

Angelica smiled as she looked down at the girl doing her pedicure and indicated her choice of nail polish colour with a sharp nod towards the one held in her left hand. She had to admit he was the only star on her books who ever said thank you for anything.

'I just wanted to remind you about your contract,' she said after only a moment's hesitation, unsure where they stood on this point. He'd been fairly adamant before he left that he wanted to think about it, and seeing the photographs of him with that woman in Croatia hadn't done anything to make her believe that he was ready to commit to another three years as DI Fierce.

'I'm still not sure,' said Leonard, whose heart was still desperate to hear from Isabella, even though he was trying to toughen himself to the idea that he would never see her again. 'As you know, I want to write songs,' he paused, unsure now if he did want to do that. 'And there are other things I might want to pursue.'

Angelica was unsurprised. She knew exactly what he might want to pursue. She'd seen the look of adoration on his face plastered all over the Daily Rag. 'Well, don't take too long,' said Angelica, deciding to go for the jugular. 'There has been a whisper that they may be looking to replace you.'

Leonard snorted. 'Ha, I don't think they'd do that. The world knows me as Detective Fierce. Who on earth could take my place?'

'Well, as I said, it's only a rumour, but I have heard the name John Elvers being bandied about,' she said evilly, knowing full well what his reaction would be.

He sat up straight, staring out of the small window of his kitchen, mind racing. He wouldn't put it past them. The young man was now headline news thanks to his ex-wife and, despite the fact he couldn't act for toffee, would be a scandalous enough replacement to ensure viewing figures. Making a decision he said firmly, 'give me 24 hours; you'll have your answer by tomorrow morning.'

That would give Isabella time to get in touch if she wanted to, he thought. If she didn't, he would know that it was over, and he could get on with his life.

Angelica agreed that she could stall them for just one more day, and fervently hoping that nothing would lure him away in the next few hours, looked down again at her feet.

'I don't like it,' she snapped at the young girl, carefully painting her nails in the shade she had requested. 'Do it again, something red I think...it better suits my mood.'

☼

Isabella spent a long time drafting her letter to Leonard. Not only did she want to let him know how she felt about him, but she also wanted to apologise for her knee-jerk reaction to the press coverage. She read, and reread, the letter several times before she felt completely happy with it. It wasn't the same as speaking to him, but it would have to do, and possibly it was easier to be honest in a Word document. When she was ready, she sent it to Derek, who promised to forward it to Angelica immediately and mark it as high priority.

That done, she called Mia to let her know that the villa was, in fact, empty and could be cleaned and prepared for the winter hibernation that vacation houses entered at this time of year. Promising that she would go the next day, Mia said she would call and let her know when it was ready for the final inspection of the year. Isabella warned her that there might be photographers lurking outside the house, which Mia seemed to find strangely exciting.

Sighing, she felt at a bit of a loss now. Isabella wondered how she was going to fill her time until Leonard responded to her. Sandy and Luka returned from their trip to the bakers, the smell of morning pastries filling the room.

'So what are we going to do today?' asked Sandy as she laid the still warm croissants on a plate.

'I'm not sure I'm up to much,' responded Isabella, taking a tentative bite from one before putting it back down and pushing her plate away.

It was another glorious day and Sandy was determined not to let her friend languish at the apartment, so she bullied her into going to the beach. 'Come on, it's not fair on Luka being cooped up all day and some fresh air will be good for you both,' she insisted. 'I, for one, am not going to sit here looking at your sadness all day!'

As they got ready, despite her miserable state, Isabella couldn't help but smile at the fact that Derek was still here, and coming along with them. He seemed to have slotted straight into Sandy's life without so much as a second thought from either of them. "I wish it was always that easy," she thought, as she feigned enthusiasm for the outing, and prepared for a day by the sea.

YESTERDAY

When Angelica arrived at her office, the next morning, she was feeling particularly perky. The new star she had been chasing had signed up with her, and she'd heard nothing from Leonard as of yet, so it seemed like another contract, and her commission, was in the bag. Sipping from her Costa coffee takeaway as her MacBook hummed to life, she started to trawl through her inbox, which, as usual, had filled up overnight.

There was one from Sublime Retreats, reporting great reactions to the Instagram posts of Leonard tagged on their feed. They were thrilled that the star had managed to time it with a scandal and were already talking about hosting another of her talents, maybe in one of their 'City Break' properties which was a new program they were developing and keen to promote in a similar fashion.

Smiling to herself, she continued to scroll through her inbox, only stopping when she saw the one from

Derek, its red exclamation mark demanding that it be read. She glanced through his message, frowning and then opened the attachment. Reading Isabella's letter, her spirits sagged. There was no way Leonard would be able to ignore this heartfelt declaration of love. Even she had felt slightly moved by it. She stared at the screen for a few moments, her mind racing through all her possible options and their outcomes. Always being a fan of the simplest, least messy options in life, she clicked on the email and marked it as spam. There, problem solved.

☼

Sure enough, an hour later, a courier arrived with the signed contract. There was no message. Leonard had found it excruciating, signing on that dotted line, it felt as if he was signing his life away. But he forced himself to go through with it and was determined to move forward and not think about Isabella if he could help it.

Finding himself with an unexpected day at home with his boys, Rennie wasn't expecting them back until tomorrow afternoon; he came up with the plan to take them to London Zoo. He didn't usually have the time, or inclination, on the odd weekend visits, to do anything in particular, so he was determined to make the most of this opportunity and make up for the fore-shortened holiday. He had made up his mind that he was going to speak to Rennie about his allotted time with them. He'd had enough of not seeing them, and by the sounds of it, she wouldn't mind a little more free time, anyway.

At London Zoo, Leonard, Alex and Ben were standing, mesmerised in front of the monkey enclosure when his phone rang. Surprised to see that it was Rennie, he had a pang of fear that she would be demanding them back today, scuppering their plans for a movie and Pizza Express.

'Good morning, Rennie,' he greeted her as calmly as he could, 'how was the honeymoon?'

'Oh, it was fantastic,' she trilled, 'nearly as good as ours!'

Shaking his head in sympathy for her new husband, he cut to the chase 'I hope you're not calling to ask me to bring the boys back today? We have got plans you know!' he could feel his temper rising already, pre-empting her request.

'Actually, no... I was kinda hoping you could keep them a little longer? Johnny has a work thing in the States and I wanted to go with him, get some shopping in. We're going to New York!'

Trying to keep the surprise and relief out of his voice, Leonard hastily responded, 'I'd love to. We're having a great time. How long were you thinking of exactly?'

'I'm not 100% sure yet. Can we keep it fluid? I'll be in touch in a couple of days so we can sort it out.'

Instantly agreeing to this vague plan, it was only after she hung up that he realised that she hadn't asked to speak to her sons. She hadn't asked about them at all, now he came to think of it.

'Dad, Dad,' called Ben excitedly, breaking into his train of thought. 'You've got to come and see this. There's a monkey throwing poo!' he shouted with glee, causing the people standing nearby to chuckle. Grinning at the boy, he went to see the spectacle that was causing so much joy, glad for the distraction from his ex-wife and the sharp, constant images of Isabella that were persistently flitting through his brain. He still couldn't believe that she hadn't been in touch... Wasn't going to be in touch.

The thought seared through his brain, causing his heart to wince with the pain. How could she be so cold? He would have to accept that no one would love him for who he was. Rennie and Isabella had both used him for their own purpose and discarded him when they were done. Another squeal of joy from the boys, as more faeces made their projectile course across the compound, brought home sharply the fact that here were two people who loved him unconditionally. And he decided there and then to focus entirely on them from now on. Who needed a love life, after all? Certainly not DI Fierce!

The next few days dragged intolerably for Isabella, each morning starting with optimism that today would be the day that he got in touch with her. But as the hours passed, and the sun made its uncaring trajectory across the sky, with no news, she sank into depression and inertia. Mia called to say that the villa was done, but even that didn't lift her spirits the way it usually did, heralding the start of her winter.

'There's an envelope for you by the way,' the maid added casually, at the end of the conversation, 'looks like your star left you a tip!'

Barely able to hold back the tears, Isabella thanked her and said she would be in touch to settle the last month's wages, before throwing her phone across the room, where it bounced off the wall, and hid back under the covers and burst into sobs. She and Luka were still staying at Sandy's. Although it seemed the press had finally cottoned on to the fact that Leonard had left, she hadn't had the energy to take them back home. She chose instead to wallow in bed, while her friend did her best to entertain Luka, occasionally checking in and force-feeding Isabella, despite her protests.

Rushing in at the new sounds of distress from her spare bedroom, Sandy stood in the doorway, looking at the shuddering heap of blankets that was her best friend. Deciding that enough was enough, she marched over and flung the covers back, revealing Isabella and her tear-stained face. Despite her best efforts at spoon-feeding her, she could see Isabella had lost weight. Her hair was matted, squashed to one side, and she looked like she hadn't slept for a year.

'Isabella Angelo, get your arse out of that bed and go and have a shower,' she insisted in a voice that brooked no argument. Grabbing a towel from the chest of drawers beside her, she threw it at Isy, who caught it reflexively.

'He... he left a tip,' she wailed up at Sandy. 'Mia says there's an envelope. After everything, he left a tip, like I was just his concierge, and nothing else.'

Slightly taken aback, that seemed a bit harsh, even for a man, but resolving to get her friend out of bed and back into the real world, she said, 'well never mind that for now, we can talk about it later. You need to sort yourself out. You have a son who misses you and a life to live. I'd also like my flat back; it's hard to have an adventurous sex life with an inquisitive kid in the next room!'

Despite her wretched state, Isabella felt the glimmer of a smile play around her mouth. It was an alien sensation. She begrudgingly rose, clutching the towel, and silently slouched out of the room. Sandy stood stock still until she heard the bathroom door close and the sound of running water. Content that her friend was doing what she was told, she stripped the bed and flung open the window to let in some fresh air and blow the fug and misery out of the room.

By the time Isabella had finished showering, washing off days of sloth and tears, she was amazed to find she did feel a little better. Pulling on some clean clothes, she ventured out into the lounge to find Sandy in the kitchen pouring coffee.

'Where's Luka?' she asked, looking around, a pang of guilt shooting through her. She had no idea where he was.

'Glad you've finally remembered you have a son,' chastised Sandy sharply, and then softened as she saw Isabella's face droop. 'He's with his grandparents,' she explained a little more gently. 'I figured you could both do with a change today. I know I could!'

Taking their cups out onto the terrace, Isabella blinking in the unaccustomed sunlight. She took a moment to take some deep, cleansing breaths and try to appreciate the beautiful day before her. Joining Sandy at the table, she glanced at her friend before saying, 'I can't thank you enough, Sandy, for everything you've done these last few days.'

'It was nothing. Someone had to look out for you,' Sandy replied, smiling at her. 'Let's face it, you've been good for nothing.'

Nodding, Isabella took a sip from her coffee, gazing out at the sea, which was having its usual calming effect on her. 'I just don't know what to do next,' she murmured. 'Usually this time of year I would be gung ho, sorting out my house and garden, happily getting ready for the winter. But now... Now my head seems stuck. I can't think further than this cup right here,' she said, waving it vaguely at Sandy.

'What you need is a plan,' Sandy stated, her tone giving evidence to the fact that she had been thinking about this. 'I want you to come and work at the restaurant for me,' she announced, looking at Isabella to see how this would be received. Startled, Isy replied, 'but you don't need anyone in the winter. You only open on weekends, unless you're doing something different this year?'

'Well, different in one aspect,' Sandy responded, a smile blossoming on her face. 'Derek and I plan to keep seeing each other. Strangely, he's not too annoying and I quite like his company,' she quipped glibly, but Isabella could see the tinge of shyness on Sandy's face and marvelled at it. Her friend had never been one for mushy stuff, but it seemed cupid had aimed his arrow well this time.

'That's wonderful news' confirmed Isabella, meaning it despite her own sorry love life, 'but I'm not sure how that distracts from the restaurant?'

'I plan to visit him in London as often as I can. I might even join him when he travels for work. As long as he's going somewhere exotic, of course!' she replied with an impish grin which was much more like the Sandy of old.

Taking this all in, Isabella tried to quash the jealousy that threatened to overtake her. Not only did Sandy have an exciting new relationship, but she was also going to travel to who knows where; it didn't seem fair. A couple of days ago, she thought she had exactly the same exciting things to look forward to, but look at her now. Stuck here, unwanted and unloved, and even her best friend wasn't going to be around as much.

Shaking her head to dislodge these strands of self-pity, which were worming their way into her usually positive spirit, she rose and went over to Sandy, giving her a heartfelt hug. 'I am so happy for you,' she said genuinely, raising her head a notch so she could look into her eyes. 'And I think working a few nights a week is a great idea. It will stop me from moping and get me out of the house. Thank you.' And she hugged her again.

Isabella settled into a dreary routine. Each day she awoke with a start, thought of him and then cried quietly in her bed for a while, before dragging herself up and into motion and beginning her day. She passed lifelessly through every 24 hours, functioning as a parent as best she could, before the relief of sleep finally overtook her in the small hours of the morning. The next morning saw her repeat the pain-filled process all over again.

She had taken up Sandy's suggestion on working for her at the weekends, and she dutifully showered and made an effort to dress nicely before going to the restaurant every Friday and Saturday night to perform her duties. To the untrained eye, the waitress who met the incoming guests at Mjesto Sastanka was a happy, cheerful woman who was eager to be of service. But those who knew her could see her steady decline, the weight loss and her pallor telling another story, and they could spot the lie that was the smile on her face.

Luka's grandparents looked sadly on while doing their best to support her, unsure of how they could best help. Ana was constantly filling the fridge with home-cooked meals in the hope she would be tempted to eat a morsel, and they took the boy every weekend to give her a break. Ivan had taken over tending the garden. Even that no longer seemed to bring her joy, and he quietly got on with making sure that the weeds didn't overwhelm the flowers and vegetables she had so lovingly tended in the past.

When Sandy returned from a ten-day trip with

Derek to Cannes, she was shocked at the deterioration of her friend.

'You look like shite,' she stated when she arrived at Isabella's house on Saturday afternoon. 'And if you lose any more weight, you'll disappear. Have you eaten today?' she demanded, stalking through to the kitchen with Isabella trailing behind her.

'Not yet. I'll grab something in a bit,' she lied. 'Coffee?' she added to distract her. Nodding, Sandy glanced around the house; the once immaculate home was looking as unloved as Isabella plainly felt.

'Actually, scrap that. Let's go out somewhere. Come on, let's drive down to Bol and get some fresh air,' she insisted as she saw Isabella start to refuse. 'We can sit by the sea and talk about life.'

Despite her lack of desire to do anything at all, Isabella conceded. She knew Sandy well enough to know she wouldn't give in, and being away from the house would be a distraction from the mountain of laundry that had piled up and taunted with her worthlessness every time she walked past. On the short drive down to the seafront, Sandy did her best to draw Isabella out of her shell, regaling with her travels and asking about the restaurant, but she could barely get out more than a syllable from her.

Once they had settled into their usual chairs at their favourite café on the seafront and placed their orders. Sandy took the bull by the horns.

'This has to stop, you know.'

'What has to stop?' Isabella answered stubbornly, not wanting to be drawn into this particular conversation.

'You know damn well what I mean, all this moping about, pining and wasting away. It doesn't suit you!' she paused, watching Isabella's face closely for a minute before driving her point home 'you weren't this much of a mess when Matteo died.'

Shocked at the sound of his name, Isabella stared at Sandy, anger and pain fleeting across her face. 'This is totally different,' she said flatly.

'How is it different?' Sandy asked gently, seeing that she had broken through a chink in the armour and wanting to force her way in deeper.

Isabella stared out to sea, watching the small waves racing into the harbour. Not finding her usual solace from it, she turned her thoughts inward. 'Matteo didn't choose to leave me, Leonard did,' she whispered as tears began to seep from her eyes and trickle their now familiar trail down her face. She grabbed a napkin from the holder on the table and jammed it into her eyes to staunch the flow.

'Yes, he did choose to leave. But only after you told him to bugger off,' stated Sandy matter-of-factly, 'and the Isabella I know doesn't take things lying down. She dusts herself off, gets back up and fights for what she wants.'

'There's no point in fighting. He doesn't want me,' answered Isabella, who had been driven mad by thoughts of chasing after him these last few weeks, and then tormented by the scenes of rejection yet again. 'He didn't respond to my message. I made my feelings bloody clear in the letter I sent, and he ignored it. Not even a word. He could have been a gentleman, even if he didn't feel the same. He could have said something. Even if it was just "thanks, but no thanks," something to show a little respect for what I thought we had.'

'Well, as I see it, you either stand up and fight for him or stand up and get on with your life,' said Sandy firmly. None of us can bear to see this ghost of you wandering around in a daze for any longer and you are going to make yourself ill. Think of Luka!'

Isabella mumbled something into her coffee but didn't elaborate until Sandy leant forward, elbows on the table 'What was that?'

'I was waiting for a sign,' announced Isabella quietly. 'I thought the universe would send me a sign,' she added defiantly at Sandy's confused expression. 'Usually, I can see the way forward. I know what to do, but... But at the moment I can't think any further than his absence.'

Sandy looked sadly on as the tears started to roll once more down Isabella's face. 'Well chuck, as we say, "you don't get owt for nowt," if you don't see the sign that you should fight for this man then you have to accept it, dust yourself off and get on with your life.'

Nodding dejectedly in her agreement with Sandy's assessment, she smiled wanly at her. 'Well, at least we have the big party tonight at the restaurant to take my mind off things,' she interjected, not wanting to think or talk about Leonard anymore.

Taking her cue, Sandy brightened. 'Yes, it's going to be a fun night,' she agreed, thinking ahead to the preparations for the evening. 'We're going to be busy, but I like it when people book the place out for a private function. They are a little more forgiving if the service is slow,' she quipped with a smile. Happy to see that Isabella looked a little more present, rather than gazing off into space sadly, they discussed the battle plan for tonight's event as they finished their coffees and by the time she was dropped back at home, Isabella felt a little lighter.

The insurmountable sense of inertia that she had been feeling was being overtaken by a determination to accept the situation, something she had not been able to do, a small part of her insisting that her happy ever after was just around the corner if she could just hang on another day. She realised she was finally, slowly but surely, coming to accept the fact that he didn't love her, as painful as that was, and she had to move on.

In London, Leonard was also trying to move on. He had kept his promise to himself and had enlisted an estate agent to look for a property for him. He was determined to find somewhere that was a real home, with a space for the boys and his studio, despite the fact he hadn't picked up his guitar since he got home. Filming had started for the next season of Fierce Conflicts, and he uncomplainingly went through the motions, arriving every day in his trench coat, without a hangover, and with an uncharacteristically pliant demeanour.

In fact, he was being so remarkably, tacitly pleasant that Angelica felt compelled to have a word with him. She arranged to meet him on the premise of discussing some possible product endorsements and they met at Gilbert Scott's for drinks on a particularly cold December afternoon. Walking into the high-ceilinged grandeur, Leonard shrugged off his trench coat, folded it over one arm and rubbed his hands together until the warmth of the room began to seep in.

Casting about, he saw Angelica sitting at the bar that stretched down one side of the restaurant, sipping her drink, and watching the diners with feline avidity in the mirror that backed it. Taking his seat easily on the high-backed stool next to hers, he indicated to the barman he would have whatever she was drinking, uninterested in what that may be. After some initial pleasantries, Angelica got down to business with her usual aplomb.

'So, we have several interesting prospects,' she asserted, reaching down and pulling some paperwork out of her bag. 'There's this clothing brand,' she pointed out, placing some advertising shots in front of him next to his glass. 'We also have a great offer from this independent whisky producer,' she continued, adding the relevant paperwork, 'and lastly...' she stated, and with a flourish laid the most lucrative option on the top of the pile. Leonard looked down at the photograph of a bottle of cologne called Rage, dispassionately.

With an airy wave of one hand, and picking up his

drink with the other, he remarked mildly, 'whichever you think is best, you're the boss' and took a sip. In the glow of the ambient lighting from the Victorian lamps along the bar, he saw her expression change briefly to one of concern before returning to her normal glare. As he savoured the quintessentially English flavours of his cocktail, was that rhubarb he could taste, maybe apple, he thought as he watched with detached amusement her struggle for something to say. It was an unusual sight, and even in his disconnected state, he was enjoying it.

'The thing is Leonard,' she finally settled on, 'you need to do some more promotion of the character. It's been weeks since you have made the news. Not since Croatia, in fact,' she finished carefully, watching for his reaction. He blanched visibly and swallowed the rest of his drink in one gulp before he plonked the glass back down without saying a word.

'Rage would be a perfect fit for DI Fierce, and it's an incredibly generous offer,' she continued, 'but not for this meek and mild person that has been wandering about for these last few weeks.' She didn't want to go into the concerns expressed by the director John, and the studio as a whole, that he had lost his edge, and his character was suffering as a result.

Leonard was enjoying the buzz from the cocktail. It was the first drink he had had since the day he got back, and he gestured to the barman to get them some more. It hadn't been a conscious decision not to drink; he just hadn't felt like it. Hadn't felt like doing much of anything. But now, with the familiar hum in his veins, he was remembering why he liked it.

'Leonard,' bleated Angelica, trying to get his attention, 'this is serious. People are talking, and not in a good way. What the hell is going on?'

'you make me so foolish, why do I feel this blueness' Leonard sang, to nobody in particular, and turning to look at her, smiled sadly at Angelica. 'I'm not sure I'm Fierce anymore, let alone Raging,' he noted with no mirth and a nod towards the artwork on the bar.

With only the briefest flicker of guilt at the disposal of the love letter, Angelica tried to reason with him. 'Leonard, you have to get back to it. Whatever this current... malaise is, you need to snap out of it and fast. If you don't, you will lose your contract with Brava TV, and you and I both know that without Detective Fierce you would be nothing,' she finished triumphantly.

The familiar refrain failed to have its usual effect, Leonard noticed dispassionately, and with a feeling of increasing lightness, as if a burden had been lifted, he stood up, his untouched drink on the bar.

'The thing is, Angelica, I no longer care,' he uttered and walked out, leaving an open-mouthed agent behind him.

At Mjesto Sastanka the atmosphere was alive with chatter and laughter, aromas of grilled meats and other creations coming out of the kitchen and wafting over the now covered terrace, its protective winter plastic shell firmly held in place against the elements.

Isabella and Sandy were running, serving the long table as quickly as they could, enjoying the family's merrymaking nearly as much as the guests' themselves. The champagne was flowing to celebrate the marriage of a beautiful young couple, who were so wrapped up in each other at the head of the table that they could have been there by themselves.

After the cake had been cut and the photographer had finally settled back down, they began to serve it gratefully, their feet beginning to protest at the intense labour of the evening. Isabella was laying down the last plates of cake, at the quieter end of the table where the older members of the family were sitting, when one of them roughly grabbed her by the arm. Looking down into the broad, dark features and bushy eyebrows of the man she had noticed staring at her earlier, and smiling in the face of his rudeness, she asked, 'can I get you something else, sir?'

'It's you, isn't it?' he challenged, standing up, his face infused with anger, and crowding her back against the wall. 'You are the kuja,' he spat, 'that broke his heart.'

Bewildered, Isabella looked around for help, but Sandy had disappeared into the kitchen and no one else seemed to be paying any attention.

'I... I'm sorry, I don't know what you are talking about,' she breathed, her eyes still darting in the hope of a lifeline. This man was obviously a little unhinged.

'They say in the papers that Fierce Conflicts will be no more. That DI Fierce is no longer fierce, his heart too broken to carry on.'

Realisation dawning, Isabella sagged against the wall for support. She had been deliberately avoiding any news of late, so had been unaware of the current furore battling in the English papers. The man was still staring at her vehemently, his face screwed up in anger. 'You killed him!' he bellowed, causing silence to fall across the terrace as everyone looked up to see what was happening and Sandy raced out from the kitchen.

'Is everything alright here?' she asked, glancing from Isy's face to that of the angry customer in confusion.

'I...' began Isabella, before being overcome with emotion and running from the room, untying her apron as she went and uncaring as her recalcitrant curls escaped from their bondage.

When Sandy came to find her a short while later, she discovered her sitting at the table outside of the kitchen, the area that the staff used to take a break when they could. Isabella was crying again, tears and mucus dribbling down her face unattractively as she looked up at Sandy's appearance.

'Here,' she said, passing her a wad of napkins to repair the damage. 'Are you OK?' she asked pointlessly.

'I was' Isabella hiccupped, 'but that man... That man told me that Leonard is heartbroken' she stammered. 'It must be a lie, another publicity stunt?' she pleaded with her friend.

'I don't know what it is, but I think you should speak to Jakov, that man in there. You might find what he has to tell you interesting' and seeing that Isabella

didn't protest, she nodded over her shoulder to someone standing in the shadows and the squat form of the
taxi driver emerged.

'I am sorry to shout,' he said quietly, as if afraid now
to raise his voice, 'but I am being very upset by this
news. I love that show and I love that man. I met him
you know when he came?'

Isabella looked at him inquiringly, as he carefully
took a seat at the table next to her. Sandy, assured that
there would be no more disturbances, left them to it
and made her way back into the restaurant to deal
with the last clearing of the befouled table and the
final orders of champagne.

Outside, a silence had fallen at the table, Isabella
waiting for this man to continue and Jakov trying to
formulate into English what he needed to say. This
girl's reaction to what he had said was not what he had
been expecting. He had assumed that she wouldn't
care. From what Leonard had told him at the airport
before he left, it had seemed that she had no feelings for him. But here she was, tear-stained, vulner-
able and fragile, looking for all the world like someone
with a broken heart. It was painful to see, and he felt
dreadful for having contributed to it.

So, slowly, he began to recount his tale. The meeting with the famous detective, rescuing him and his
boys on arrival when they lost their car and saving
the day again when they got stuck on Hvar, Isabella
nodding – that little mystery finally solved. Finally, he
came to the sad, final meeting, when he'd driven Leonard to the airport, and what the man had told him

whilst they waited for the delayed plane to arrive.

'So you see,' he finished, 'he loves you. He believes that you don't feel the same, so he went home.' Isabella absorbed the information which pounded into her brain like a tattoo. "If he loved her, why didn't he answer her letter? Maybe he hadn't believed her?" Shaking her head in dismissal of this thought, she couldn't have made her feelings plainer. She looked at Jakov and whispered, 'I wrote to him, told him everything, and told him I loved him. If he loved me, as you say, he would have written back.' And she stood up sadly, with a last glance at him, and trailed wearily inside to help Sandy finish clearing up.

The guests departed, in dribs and drabs, merrily making their way out the door as the girls worked to get the restaurant back to its usual state, the discussion of tonight's news being shelved for when they had finished work, an unspoken agreement. When they had finally rearranged the tables and chairs into their usual positions and said goodnight to the rest of the staff, Isabella collapsed onto a chair, exhausted. She was rung out mentally and physically and looked like a rag doll flung to one side after play. Walking back from the bar, Sandy waved a bottle of champagne at her, the two flute glasses casually gripped in her other hand.

'I think we deserve some of this,' she announced as she plopped down wearily on the chair next to her and proceeded to skilfully twist the cork open. They sat in silence, watching as the golden bubbles danced up the side of the glasses, then settled back down, foaming gently in understated anticipation.

'To a good night's work,' Sandy proffered her glass towards Isabella, who reached forward slightly to grasp her drink and raised it briefly to acknowledge the toast before taking a sip. Catching an errant bubble that was trailing down the side of her glass with her finger, Sandy idly ran it around the rim, causing a faint hum to fill the silence.

'Can you stop that?' growled Isabella, holding her glass with stressed, white fingers. Afraid of what might be about to snap, Sandy pulled her hand away as if scalded and challenged, 'So come on then. What's going on in the curly-headed brain of yours? I thought you would be happy with the news brought by our bushy-eyed Hermes?'

'Huh,' she countered, 'I don't see that it makes any difference,' she replied gloomily, but Sandy could see there was a question in her eyes.

'Why not?' She probed, trying to understand exactly what was going on in Isabella's head.

'Even if some of what Jakov said was true, let's say Leonard did have some feelings for me when he left. The fact that he didn't respond to my letter tells me that something's changed, or he decided it wasn't worth it, or maybe he found someone else.'

Unused to seeing Isabella so self-deprecating, Sandy played Devil's advocate. 'Well, what if none of those things is true? What if...' she cast about for an example, 'what if he didn't get the letter? That would explain his silence, wouldn't it?'

'It was an email, not a carrier pigeon! The chances

of it going astray are minimal' Isabella retorted. 'And besides,' she added, rummaging in her bag, 'he wouldn't have left this!' she pronounced, pulling out a tattered-looking envelope with Sublime Retreats tastefully emblazoned along the bottom. 'You don't leave a tip for someone you love' she fumed, 'that was the biggest insult of all!'

Sandy laughed mirthlessly. 'I can't believe you haven't spent that! Carrying it around is a bit odd, babe, and probably not helping the healing process. I think it's time to let it go.'

'You know what, you're right,' exclaimed Isabella as she started to tear the top of the envelope. 'This has been holding me back. Taunting me every time I look through my bag! Well, enough is enough,' and with a last tug, the small envelope came apart and its contents fluttered to the floor.

Both women looked down and stared in surprise. Bending down slowly, Isabella picked up the photograph first, holding it up to see it properly in the candlelight. Happy smiling faces looked back at her, and she bit down a cry. She knew how much Ben loved his photos, and he'd left one for her.

Passing it to Sandy in silence, she reached down again for the piece of paper that had floated down under the table. Ignoring the glancing blow to her head as she sat back up, she began to read. As it dawned on her what she was holding and she read the lyrics, beginning to understand their meaning, she started to feel dizzy and her hand flew to her mouth in shock.

'What is it?' Sandy asked, worried by the colour

draining from Isabella's face, and when she didn't answer she echoed 'what is it, Isy?'

Isabella looked up; her face charged with emotions and her eyes shimmering in the subdued light, she whispered, 'it's the sign.'

☼

Leonard was viewing yet another potential property, this time in the wilds of the Yorkshire moors. This had become his life now. Every weekend he had appointments lined up all across the country in his bid to find his retreat, and he had to admit he was enjoying the travelling around. He'd opted to go by train, rather than arrange a car, and the freedom of it was wonderful. It had been a long time since he had been a member of the general public and wrapped up in his big coat and a hat and scarf against the biting wind, he slotted right in and only occasionally got spotted by a fan.

As he wandered around the old farmhouse he was currently viewing, he had to admit it was a magnificent property, with views of rolling dales on three sides. He could see the estate agent standing out in the garden, her mobile clamped to her ear as she tried to have a conversation over the noise of the wind. He knew she was getting fed up with him. He couldn't remember how many places he'd seen now, but none of them had been quite right. He watched as she finished her call and came back towards the house, disappearing from view for a moment until the front door opened and she was blown in with a rush of cold air.

She looked at him hopefully, rubbing life into her hands 'Well, Mr Lupine? What do we think of this one?'

'We,' he said sarcastically, 'think it's a wonderful place.' And he watched her face light up. 'But it's not the one,' he added, taking a little sadistic pleasure in watching her face droop again.

'What's wrong with this one?' she demanded. He could tell she was near the end of her professional tether. The kudos of house hunting with the famous detective seemed to have worn off. 'It has the right number of bedrooms,' she insisted. 'It has a separate annexe for your studio. It's remote with fantastic views. In fact, it ticks every box on your wishlist' she was almost wailing at this point.

'I don't know what to tell you,' he said. 'It is all of those things, but it's not the right one. I will know it when I see it; I will feel it when I walk in. It will lift my spirits and inspire me. It will comfort me and welcome me; I just know I will know when it's right.' He shrugged, unable to express his feelings any further.

With a deep sigh, she looked at her clipboard. 'Well, let's move on then, shall we? I have a few more I can show you in the area today and some further south tomorrow.' And she spun on her heels and marched out, leaving Leonard to trial in her wake.

That night, as he settled into bed in the comfortable Bed and Breakfast he had booked into, he leafed through the sheets of property information he had collected today and glanced through the ones lined up for tomorrow. There were some nice-looking houses, but he was starting to despair ever finding the right one. Nothing seemed to grab him. There was always a missing element. His phone rang, and putting the papers to one side, he stretched over and picked it up off the bedside table, surprised to see it was Rennie's home number.

'Hi, how are you?' he answered blandly, wondering what on earth the wretched woman wanted now.

'Dad, it's me,' came a small voice. Leonard sat up straight. 'Alex, is that you? Is everything OK?'

'Yes, dad it's OK. We are just lonely and we wanted to talk to you,' his son said.

'Well, it's lovely to talk to you, but why are you lonely? Where's Mum?'

'I'm not sure. We haven't seen her for a couple of days. There is a new nanny' he added, 'but she doesn't speak English, so it's kinda hard talking to her' he said diplomatically.

Leonard was furious. He could feel his anger rising and was doing everything he could to hold it down. He had asked Rennie repeatedly in these last weeks to let him have the boys at the weekends, thinking they would enjoy the adventure of travelling around with him to look at potential homes, but she had constantly fobbed him off, claiming they had other engagements, and making them sound like family ones.

Making a decision there and then, he promised the boy 'Daddy will come down tomorrow morning to see you, OK? I'm up in Yorkshire at the moment but I will get up early and get down to you as quickly as I can.'

'Really? Oh thanks, Dad, it will be great to see you.' Leonard smiled as he could hear Ben in the background squeaking like a racoon, 'put your brother on for a bit before he explodes', he laughed.

As he lay there later, unable to sleep, he planned the conversation he was going to have with Rennie as soon as he got the chance. It was two months now since they'd returned from Croatia, and it seemed that nothing had changed. She was still an absent parent, and still unable to provide suitable care for her sons. It was deplorable. The train schedule informed him that the first train left at 5.30 am and he was going to be on it. Looking at his watch and seeing it was nearly two already, he tried to settle down to sleep.

FEELS LIKE HOME

Jakov sat in his seat, gripping the armrests for dear life, as the engines roared and the plane rolled down the runway, inexorably picking up speed until the stomach-lurching moment when the wheels lifted off the ground. He remained tensed up for a few minutes until he adjusted to the sensation and then looked around proudly as if he had been responsible for the safe takeoff through sheer willpower.

He had never left his home country before; the idea of going on a plane was terrifying to him. But the plight of his favourite star had compelled him to take action, and he cast his fears, if not aside, then at least shoved them to the back of his mind where he could try and ignore their cries.

He gratefully ordered a whisky when the stewardess trundled down the aisle and felt his body relax and braved a look out of the window. Feeling slightly dizzy at the sight of land so far below him, tiny dots that must surely be houses, impossibly small, he adjusted his glance back to the front of the cabin and mused about the journey ahead. He didn't have a concrete plan, he just knew he had to find Leonard and talk some sense into him.

Not being computer savvy, he had enlisted the help of one of his nephew's to track down the location of the studios where the infamous detective show was filmed. He smiled. He was being a bit of a detective himself. He just hoped he would be as successful in his quest as DI Fierce always was on his.

As the train chugged into London on a misty Sunday morning, Leonard was feeling weary but thrilled to be going to see his boys. Looking at the grimy map on the tube station wall, he remembered that Gloucester Road was the nearest point to his old house and once he'd figured out where he would need to change trains, got his ticket from the machine and easily found the escalator that would take him to the right platform.

The chilly ten-minute walk from the station did an amazing job of waking him up, and he jogged up the stairs to the familiar front door, the backdrop to Rennie's artful announcement not so long ago. He heard Ben and Alex racing down the stairs in response to his knock and the door was flung open in delight, the pyjama-clad children flinging themselves at him, gripping him like an octopus clamping onto a rock. Once he had detangled from their clasp, he made his way through to the kitchen; the boys chattering animatedly as they scampered after him.

'So where's the nanny?' he asked casually whilst the kettle was boiling for his tea, and he helped them take the bowls down from the cupboard for their cereal.

'Oh, she's not up yet,' Alex replied, shrugging, as if this was to be expected. 'She's not really a morning person.'

Choosing not to respond to this, Leonard made another snap decision. 'I tell you what, after breakfast, you can get some things together and come and stay with me for a few days. Would you like that?' Their beaming faces were answer enough, but then doubt flickered across Alex's face.

'What about school, Dad?' he said earnestly. 'We still have a few more days until the end of term,' before spooning a heap of Cheerios into his mouth.

'Don't worry about that,' Leonard said, knowing full well that the last few days before Christmas were more about parties, plays and the teachers having a crafty snifter in the staff room if memory served him correctly. 'You can come and watch my last day of filming tomorrow; you'd like that wouldn't you? And then we can get ready for Christmas.'

Pleased with his plan, Leonard drained his tea and took the boys upstairs to pack. It felt strange being back in this house. He felt like an intruder, but he ignored the sensation and hastened to get them organised.

'Here's my bag,' said Ben, handing him the plane-studded backpack that he had used for their holiday.

Leonard stared at it stupidly, flashbacks of Croatia and Isy halting his course. 'Are you OK Dad?' asked Ben, unsure why his father had stopped moving, or talking for that matter.

'Yes, yes, I'm fine, Benny; let's get some clothes together, shall we?' Leonard asked, forcing his mind back to the present.

They were just about to leave when a bleary-faced young girl came up from the basement, where the nanny's quarters were, and looked at them in confusion.

Leonard handed her the note that he had scribbled out for Rennie and said, 'The boys are coming to stay with me for a few days' and watched her carefully, looking for some sign of understanding. Her small face screwed up in concentration, and she shook her head.

'Use your phone, Dad, use the translate thing. She speaks Polish' said Ben helpfully, 'that's how we have been talking to her!' "Thank God for modern technology," Leonard thought and promptly tapped out the sentence into his phone and showed it to the girl. Nodding, she muttered 'OK' and trailed off into the kitchen, obviously unconcerned by this turn of events.

Happy with that, they left for Leonard's apartment, stopping at Waitrose on the way to stock up on supplies and goodies for the next couple of days. He had already placed an online order for their expected Christmas visit, but his usual diet of cheese and crackers would not satisfy the boys until then. Back at the flat, he happily unpacked the shopping and he carefully put everything away as the boys upended their small bags in his bedroom, their version of unpacking.

A vision flashed across his mind of Isabella there with them, smiling and helping him, all of them looking forward to the festive period together, and he stamped down on it hard before it overtook him. He wasn't going to let thoughts of that woman spoil these next days with his sons.

He was up early the next day, thankful for the last day of filming and delighted to be sharing it with the boys. He couldn't believe he had never thought to bring them along before, and as the morning progressed, he was happy that he finally had. Seeing the whole process through their eyes brought some of the magic back to his usually humdrum workday. Even the simple act of getting lunch from the catering van that served the set was wondrous to them, the fact that you could choose whatever you liked and didn't have to pay kept them running back up for more until they were quite bloated.

'I won't be needing to feed you two tonight,' Leonard joked as they made their way back to the makeup area so he could be made ready for the final, blood-splattered scene.

'Mr Lupine' called one of the security guards, hurrying to catch up with him. 'Mr Lupine, there's a man at the gate. He says he's a friend of yours? He wants to come in and see you.' Perplexed, Leonard looked around and towards the hut that guarded the entrance to the lot. In the distance, he could see a short man waving energetically at him. There was something familiar about the barrel shape that prompted him to start towards the entrance, and as he drew closer, the beaming face of Jakov came into view.

'Mr Lupine! Mr Lupine! I have come from Croatia to see you!' bellowed the man in his thrill at seeing his favourite detective once more.

'Jakov!' Leonard exclaimed, shaking him warmly by the hand across the security barrier. 'What an amazing surprise. What on earth are you doing here?

Looking suspiciously around, Jakov leant in and muttered seriously, 'we can't talk now. The people, they will hear, but I need to tell you about the girl.' Taking Leonard's look of alarm as one of confusion, he added, 'the English girl, the one that stole your heart.'

Leonard's heart was racing, pounding her name with every beat; he had been doing so well, avoiding thinking about her. Distracting himself, first with house-hunting, and now having the boys with him had helped him get through these last days without sinking into a mire of misery. It was only at night that he allowed his mind the luxury of being tormented by thoughts of her, images flying across his mind and thoughts of 'what if?' teasing him as he imagined a million scenarios where things had ended differently.

'Is she OK?' he demanded 'Is Isabella OK?' almost shouting as anxiety took hold of him.

Shaking his bear-like head sadly, eyebrows in overdrive, Jakov responded conspiratorially, 'she is not good, Mr Lupine.'

Imagination running wild with all the terrible things that could have befallen her in his absence,

Leonard was saved from madness only by Jakov's next statement. 'She is miserable. Heartbroken!' he pronounced proudly as if this state of affairs was all his doing.

'Leonard, we need you on set,' a runner called, anxiously looking at her watch. 'We need you ready for the last scene like 5 minutes ago!' Twisting one way then the other, Leonard was unsure what to do. He desperately wanted to find out what was happening with Isabella, but he knew he had to complete his day's filming.

'Jakov, come with me,' he decided, waving the man in and walking swiftly towards the makeup section, with Jakov and the boys trailing behind him. Throwing himself into the chair, where Hayley was waiting, brushes in hand to get him ready, he called over his shoulder, 'talk to me after I finish. You can stay and watch the filming.'

Jakov's face lit up like a halogen lamp. This was beyond his wildest dreams. Imagine him, here in England, watching the mighty DI Fierce being filmed!

When John finally called 'that's a wrap' several hours later, everyone involved was exhausted. The crew from the endless retakes, Leonard had been so distracted he'd been unable to keep his lines straight, and Jakov and the boys from the nail-biting thrill of watching the action take place live. The rooftop chase ending with a spectacular fight had them all on the edge of their seats, no matter how many times they saw it filmed.

As Leonard flopped back into the chair to have the

blood and gore removed from him, he relaxed a little, relief that it was over flooding him, followed by the urgent desire to know what was happening on Brač. Wiping the last dredges of gunk off with a towel, he nodded at Hayley with thanks as she moved away.

They waited until they were in the warmth and security of the car that took them slowly through the afternoon traffic to Leonard's apartment, and the taxi driver recounted his tale of his meeting with Isabella, his shame at making her cry and her belief that Leonard didn't love her and had ignored her email.

'But she didn't send me anything! I would know. I checked everything, every day, for weeks,' Leonard argued. 'How could she think I wouldn't respond?'

'How could you think she doesn't love you?' responded Jakov sagely, 'the poor woman is beside herself with grief.'

Leonard could not believe what he was hearing. Having hardened his heart to the fact that she didn't want him in her life, he was now being pulled back into the land of hope, where anything might be possible.

'I have to go to her,' he declared urgently, making yet another snap decision. 'When we get home, I'll get online and organise flights,' he announced to the smiling faces around him.

Barely registering the lack of photographers outside his apartment, but not paying much attention as he led them into his flat, he raced into the kitchen and opened his MacBook to Google flights. He quickly found that EasyJet was flying out later that night and booked four seats to Split. When he looked up, he realised the boys had been busy and were cooking pizzas in the oven and there was a glass of wine sitting unnoticed next to him.

'Right, we're all set. I'll book a taxi then we're ready to go,' he said happily, taking a much-needed sip and smiling at Jakov. 'Thank you, my friend, for coming to rescue me,' he said sincerely. 'You have no idea what this means to me.'

'I think I do. I can see the look on your face,' grinned Jakov happily. 'It was my destiny!' he added dramatically, making them all laugh.

'I just have one more call to make,' he explained, standing up with his phone, and walking through to the bedroom to call Angelica. Standing by the window, looking out at the rooftops, he took a deep breath, preparing himself for the conversation, before hitting the speed dial and listening to its distant ringing.

'Darling!' she answered after a few rings 'how was the last day of filming? Did everything go to schedule?'

'Yes, yes, it went fine,' he said quickly, wanting to get to the point of the call. 'Angelica, can you tell me anything about an email from Derek James? An email that had a letter attached, for me?'

'Derek who?' she stalled, panic flaring and mind racing.

'Derek James, the photographer you sent to Croatia to photograph me and the boys,' he replied as calmly as he could. Her bejewelled hand was patently obvious in that occurrence. Now he'd actually thought about it, he was amazed he hadn't spotted it sooner.

'Ah.' She said carefully, not sure how much he knew.'oh yes, I remember him vaguely,' she said airily as if it was of no consequence. 'But I don't recall an email, darling. I'm sure if I had seen something that was meant for you, I would have passed it along. You know I always have your best interests at heart,' she added, almost pleadingly. Despite his lack of newsworthiness these recent months, he was still one of her biggest earners.

'All I "know"' he said, emphasising the word with vitriol, 'is that the woman I love tried to get in touch with me via you and I didn't get the message. And the only "interests" you have at heart are your own. I think we have come to the end of our road Angelica, my lawyer will be in touch.'

And he cut the call to the sound of her spluttering response. He slumped onto the bed, pushing aside the discarded Mr Kernuffle, shaking slightly. Angelica had been a necessary evil in his life for so long. Cutting her loose was terrifying. He sat for a while, contemplating what he had just done, but then Isabella's face swam into view and he smiled. Standing up with a sense of purpose, he strode into the lounge; he could worry about his career later. Right now, he was going to focus on winning back the woman he loved.

Isabella was having dinner with Sandy and Derek

while Luka had a sleepover with his grandparents. She had been so confused since she'd seen the contents of the envelope. Her romantic heart believed it was the sign she was waiting for, but her practical nature tamped down her immediate urge to fly into his arms.

'I can get you his number again, Isy,' said Derek, pouring red wine into her glass on the table. 'You could just call him.' He added pragmatically, walking over to where Sandy was standing by the cooker, stirring the Čobanac that Isabella had brought for them, and topping up her glass, his arm sliding easily around her. As the stew warmed on the stove, its paprika-rich scent filled the air and calmed her trembling spirit; Isabella took a sip of her wine and shook her head.

'I need to see him. This is not a conversation to be had with thousands of miles between you'

'Well, get on a bloody plane and go and see him!' Sandy insisted, turning around to face Isabella. Her friend's hesitation over these last few days had been driving her mad. Placing the lid on the pot, she walked over to the table and, putting her glass down, she placed her hands firmly on the surface as she bent forward to look into Isabella's concerned face.

'We can help Ivan and Anna look after Luka,' she said with a quick glance at Derek to confirm he had no objections. 'Get your arse in gear, book a flight and go tell him how you feel. It's not rocket science!'

'But what if he won't see me?' stammered Isabella. 'I was foul to him.'

'Well... Well then, you will know where you stand

and that'll be that. But one thing I've learnt in these last few weeks' Sandy said as she walked over with a smile to Derek, 'is when you get the opportunity for love, you should grab it with both hands,' and she gave the unresisting man a heartfelt kiss.

Sitting on the terrace after they had finished their meal, Isabella was still running through Sandy's plan in her mind. As terrifying as it was, she knew she was going to have to do it. She could hear the couple inside, laughing together as they cleared away the dishes, their companionable banter interspersed with squeals from Sandy as they goofed around. "I want that," she thought, "and I want it with Leonard," she confirmed.

As she picked up her phone to start looking at flights, she became aware of the sound of a guitar-playing somewhere on the street below. Smiling at the universe's timely reminder of Leonard, she stood up and wandered over to the railings to look down to see where the sound was coming from. Before her brain could register what her eyes were seeing, the familiar strains of his song floated up to her. Looking down in disbelief as he poured out his heart in the song she now knew he had written for her, she gazed at Leonard through tear-filled eyes, unable to move.

When the song came to an end he stood for a moment looking up, the sight of her a balm to his tortured heart, before calling up 'Isabella, can you forgive me?'

'Why didn't you answer me?' she voiced tremulously, the question that had been driving her to distraction since he left.

'I didn't get your message, Isy; I would never ignore anything you sent to me, please, you must know that. My bloody agent didn't forward your letter. She was afraid I would throw everything away and come running to you. And she was right.'

She reacted in a heartbeat, flying back through the kitchen, startling Sandy and Derek, before hurtling down the stairs into his arms.

HAPPY EVER AFTER

Standing on the terrace of Sea View Cottage and looking at the pool where the boys were playing, Isabella rubbed her stomach in response to the motion she felt there. Looking down as her hand soothed the kicking, she whispered, 'that's ok little girl. It won't be long now and you can come and play with your brothers.'

'Alex' she called, 'can you go and drag your dad out from the studio? Lunch is nearly ready.' She waited a moment to check that he had heard her before walking back into their house. There had been a few changes since they'd bought it six months ago.

Her wind chimes now danced happily on the terrace and her scented candles, dotted around the lounge, filled the room with their perfume. The walls and surfaces were filled with the artwork she had collected from their recent travels through Europe, but pride of place was given to the Grammy award Leonard had been awarded for 'Clueless', the first single released from his debut album.

As the boys in her life traipsed in, she smiled at them as her heart filled with love. She still couldn't believe how lucky she was. This thought reminded her of this afternoon's event and she said, 'right you three, eat up quickly and go and have a shower. We need to be at Mjesto Sastanka by four. Sandy will kill me if we are late!'

When they pulled up outside the restaurant later, Isabella took in the decorations, the pale pink and cream bunting artfully matching the flowers that framed the doorway in a skillfully woven arch; she couldn't quite believe this was happening. She left the boys to go and take their seats on the terrace and walked out through the kitchen back to the rest area, tented for the occasion, and found Sandy sitting in front of a large mirror, putting the finishing touches to her makeup. Smiling at her in the reflection, Sandy stood to greet her.

'You look stunning,' said Isabella. 'That dress is just perfect.'

Sandy smiled shyly, and did a mock twirl to cover her embarrassment, the silver sheath shimmering as she turned. Just then, her ex-husband, who was giving her away, came in brandishing a bottle of champagne.

'Ladies, I believe it is time to celebrate?' he asked with a loving smile at Sandy, who nodded eagerly and laughed as he deliberately opened it with a loud pop, hastily picking up a glass so as not to waste too much.

Once all three glasses were filled, they held them aloft. 'What shall we toast to?' he asked. The two women smiled at each other, their unexpected journeys over this last year flashing between them in an instant. 'To love' they responded in unison.

Acting as Maid of Honour, Isabella stepped in time behind Sandy, as she made her way down the aisle created by rows of chairs out on the terrace. The sunlight glinted off the dress as Josip, pausing to kiss her cheek, handed her to an awestruck Derek. Taking the small bouquet from the bride, Isabella took her place to one side and looked across the small gathering of smiling faces. She caught Jakov's eye as he gave her an enthusiastic thumbs up from his seat next to Leonard and smiled as the officiary began the ceremony.

As she felt the warmth of the sun on her back, a gentle breeze suddenly ruffled her curls, and Matteo sprang to mind. He was smiling at her, nodding his head approvingly, and she felt a sense of peace she hadn't realised she had been yearning for. Tears pricked her eyes, so she took a deep breath to restrain them, and looking up to the sky, thanked the universe for everything it had given her.

AFTERWORD

Thank you so much for reading my book. I hope you enjoyed it as much as I enjoyed the time spent bringing it all together!

As a savvy shopper you will know the importance of reviews. Please take a moment to share your thoughts with me on Amazon, Goodreads or where ever you like to hang out.

Amazon US
Amazon UK
Goodreads
BookBub

BOOKS IN THIS SERIES

Sublime Retreats Romances

This is the 2nd book in a standalone series of Romantic Escape novels that can be read in any order. They're uplifting, heartwarming stories of love, romance, hope, new beginnings and second chances featuring different characters in beautiful locations.

Begin a Romantic Escape today!

Corfu Capers

Five people, three secrets, one planned proposal. What could possibly go wrong?

For divorcée Kate Delaney, it's time to show the world that she can get along just fine without a man.

Embracing her son's desire to propose to his girlfriend with her usual overzealous planning, she organizes a vacation to Corfu and plots the 'big moment'.

But when her plans start to fall apart, she is thrown together with the dashing Pericles and is surprised to find herself relaxing into the Greek way of life.

Can this holiday really be about to change her future, and offer her a second chance of love?

Falling In Florence

Sofia Marino is focused on one thing, finding the ideal job…

When she lands the opportunity to work for Peter Williams at Sublime Retreats, it's a dream come true and the last thing on her mind is romance.

But she has to go to Florence with the cold and stand-offish Adam Flynn, and she knows she will have to discover a way to put up with him for two entire weeks.

Determined to rise to the challenge, she throws herself into making the trip successful and dragging Adam out of his shell.

As the sparks begin to fly and Florence seduces them both, will Adam let his guard drop despite his father's concerns about Sofia's family ties, and has she finally found a man she can conquer her fears for?

Discover your new favourite romance story today…

KEEP IN TOUCH

Want to keep in touch? You can sign up for my newsletter on my website: joyskye.com, for a chance to win a copy of one of the new books, and updates on new releases.

To check out my socials:

Facebook @JoySkyeAuthor
Instagram @joys.kye
Twitter @JoySkye4
BookBub Joy Skye

Printed in Great Britain
by Amazon

78145999R00150